EVIL LIVES AMONG US

A Novel by

John W. Gemmer

CCB Publishing
British Columbia, Canada

Evil Lives Among Us: A Novel

Copyright ©2020 by John W. Gemmer
ISBN-13   978-1-77143-419-5
First Edition

Library and Archives Canada Cataloguing in Publication
Title: Evil lives among us / a novel by John W. Gemmer.
Names: Gemmer, John W., 1948- author.
Identifiers: Canadiana (print) 20200236113 | Canadiana (ebook) 20200236121 |
ISBN 9781771434195 (softcover) | ISBN 9781771434201 (PDF)
Classification: LCC PS3607.E55 E95 2020 | DDC 813/.6—dc23

Cover artwork: Watercolor of forest crime scene –
          by Cheryl Ringler, Syracuse, Indiana.

Publisher: CCB Publishing
             British Columbia, Canada
             www.ccbpublishing.com

Dedication

This book is being dedicated to all the victims' families associated with violent crimes committed by serial killers.

Acknowledgements

Thanks to Kevin Sheets, and Hope Heritz, for their help and encouragement and to John Stone, who helped provide me with story ideas and information about the locale in Arkansas. Special thanks also to Jeff Rasley, my editor, and Paul Rabinovitch, my publisher, CCB Publishing, British Columbia, Canada.

Books by John W. Gemmer

The Last Assignment

Harsh Consequences

Terrorists in the Heartland

Evil Lives Among Us

Preface

Edgar Allan Poe wrote, **"The scariest monsters are the ones that lurk within our souls."** Do you believe he was right? I do.

According to the statistical information compiled by the Federal Bureau of Investigation, there are at least 2,000 serial killers roaming around the United States at any time hunting for their next victims. It's a scary thought, isn't it?

While sitting at my laptop writing this fictional story about serial killing, I began to wonder why I am so fascinated with this type of crime. Perhaps it is due to reading countless novels, watching many television shows, and viewing numerous movies about murder. Alas, it seems that murder has become part of my existence.

I do not admit to flashbacks, doubt, confusion, or paranoia, while writing this book. I simply admit that contemplating murders has become natural and interesting to me. And I would hope that, not only those attracted to the macabre, and those with a slight personality disorder, but even normally healthy readers will be drawn in to this frightening, puzzling, and entertaining tale of serial murder.

But, dear reader, don't be scared away by this Poe-like Introduction. Read on to discover the suspenseful twists and turns the story takes. By the end of the book, if you are troubled and scared thinking about the possibility that it could happen to you or someone you know, then I have done my job.

EVIL LIVES AMONG US

Chapter 1

It was a beautiful, sunny day, as Special Agent Frank Giordano drove onto the I-95 South ramp, heading towards Quantico, Virginia, from Washington, D.C. The birds were chirping and the boxwood, magnolia, and cherry trees were already in bloom. Not unusual for a typical day in early April 2004. FBI agent Giordano, was going to the United States Federal Bureau of Investigation Training Academy located 40 miles southwest from the nation's capitol. The FBI facility is located in Quantico, Virginia, on a 547-acre United States Marine Corps base.

On occasion, particularly when Frank was on a road trip, he thought about his former partner, Neil Johnson. Johnson was a good-looking, tall, African American, who was young, smart, and always impeccably dressed. He wondered about Neil's motivation for helping Al-Qaeda. What turned him against the United States? Frank found it hard not to dwell on the thought that Neil could have been, should have been, a great agent, and a good man. Johnson refused to cooperate with the authorities after he was captured. He would probably spend the rest of his life in a federal super-maximum penitentiary, Frank mused. You're not going to get paroled when treason is one of the offenses you're convicted of. Frank just couldn't understand the man. What a waste!

Giordano shrugged off his thoughts about his ex-partner, took another sip of coffee, and concentrated on driving. He knew that terrorists' motives might never be fully understood. The Bureau had developed several theories about Johnson's, but they hadn't been able to corroborate them. Why a first-class agent like Neil had become a traitor and accomplice to terrorists essentially remained a mystery.

Giordano was scheduled for an 11:00 a.m. interview with the Director of the Agent's Training Academy that included the Behavioral Science Unit (BSU) at Quantico. Frank had been transferred back to FBI headquarters in downtown Washington, D.C. after completing his assignment in Grand Rapids, Michigan. The transfer was a reward for his counter-terrorism accomplishments and dedication to duty during the past several years. He and Marie were excited about the move back to the Washington, D.C. area. But they decided not to purchase another home, until after he was officially notified of his next assignment.

Giordano knew his family was proud of his most recent accomplishments for the Bureau and for his former job with the NCIS. Frank had been a U.S. Naval officer and worked undercover in the Criminal Investigative Division. He had grown up around the law enforcement community and was proud of following in his father's footsteps. The

Giordano clan had all grown up in New Jersey and his Dad was formerly a beat cop for over 30-years on the Morristown, New Jersey, Police Department. Originally, the Giordano family hailed from Italy, specifically the region known as Calabria in the far southeastern corner of the country. The locals refer to the area as the Heel of the Boot. The Giordanos lived not far from the larger coastal community of Locri, high above the water. His relatives grew up in the mountains over-looking the town of Locri in a small agrarian village that had spectacular views of the Ionian Sea. Frank's father told him that one of his uncles had been a police officer in Naples for several decades. Frank wondered whether his own work ethic and interest in policing originated, not just from his immediate family, but also from his hard-working relatives back in Italy.

After spending years in the counter-terrorism division of the Bureau, Frank wanted a change and the BSU had drawn his attention. He realized after moving back to Virginia that his interests not only involved catching criminals, but also the psychology underlying criminal behavior. The BSU was founded at the FBI Academy in 1972. To qualify to serve in the unit, FBI applicants need at least a decade of field experience, fluency in a foreign language, have a degree in criminology, and possess a Masters in Forensic Psychology. Military experience was also a plus on an agent's application. There are over a dozen different curricula that the BSU teaches, researches, and consults about. The term "serial killer" was first coined by the BSU and it is where "criminal investigative analysis" and "profiling" were developed.

The Behavioral Science Unit seemed like a perfect fit

for Frank's training, education, experience, and interests. His undergraduate major was criminology and he had a Master's degree in forensic psychology, which he had earned several years prior to 9/11 at an Arlington, Virginia, community college. He earned his Masters while working for the Bureau. Frank decided that, if he was ever going to utilize his psychology degree, now was the time to do it. At best, he had another 15 years to work for the Bureau before retirement.

As he put down the window to throw out his partially smoked cigarette, Giordano could smell the fresh and fragrant odors of spring in the rural, Virginia air. He coughed briefly after smelling the fragrances and quickly put up the window. Frank reminded himself that it was time to start taking his allergy medication again. Giordano had an extraordinary sense of smell, which could be useful in crime detection. The downside was a susceptibility to allergies.

The familiar wooded, hilly terrain of northern Virginia began to stir his memory. He was not far from the Marine Corps base. It had been years since he had been back to Quantico. A black and white rectangular road sign alerted Frank that the base was a few miles ahead.

When he arrived at the Marine Corps base, Giordano pulled up to the guard shack and handed his identification and appointment papers to a heavily armed sentry.

"I see you are going to the BSU," said the sentry.

"Yes, hopefully I'll be working for them in the not too distant future," Frank replied. While waiting for the guard to return, he noticed that security at the facility had been enhanced since he'd been on base; undoubtedly because of 9/11. The guards used mirrors to inspect the underside of his vehicle. A military policeman with a dog circled his car. He presumed the dog was sniffing for bombs.

Seconds later, the sentry returned and said, "Good luck, Agent," as he waved Giordano through the gate.

Once inside the base, Frank found it was only a several minute drive to the FBI administration building. He parked his sedan in the visitor's lot, walked to the front door, and went inside. He was met by several armed guards in front of an enhanced x-ray security machine. Giordano was instructed to walk through the machine, in order to gain admission into the building. His briefcase was placed on a conveyor belt and was scanned. One of the sentries removed the briefcase from the conveyor and personally inspected what was inside. Not far from the security check-point, inside the foyer, was an information desk, where a young, smartly dressed woman was seated. The sign on the front of her desk was marked "Check-In". Frank showed his identification papers to the woman and she directed him to the BSU Director's office, located on the fifth floor. It was 10:30 a.m. Frank's appointment was not until 11:00. He checked in with the Director's secretary, who reminded him of Betty White, the 80-plus-year-old talented actress and well-known comedian. She politely invited him to wait in the outer office on the couch. A minute later, she appeared and offered him a cup of coffee. At precisely 11:00 a.m. the secretary notified Giordano that the Director was ready to meet with him.

It was rumored that Randolph P. Underwood was finally going to retire in the near future. Underwood was an icon at the FBI. He had been around for more than four decades and had served in many upper echelon positions at the Bureau. He was involved with almost every high-level investigation, including the Marilyn Monroe suicide investigation in 1962, the John F. Kennedy assassination in 1963, the Martin Luther King, Jr. and the Robert F. Kennedy assassinations in 1968, the Ronald Reagan attempted assassination in 1981, 9/11, and, of course, the famous, Robert Hanssen, FBI spy case, just to name a few. Hanssen was the agent who sold top secret United States government documents to the Soviet Union and was caught in 2001.

In early 1999, Underwood was asked to take the position by Louis Freeh, the former FBI Director. Underwood was also encouraged to accept the appointment by his long-time friend and fellow alumnus of Yale University, United States President William J. Clinton. Randolph Underwood postponed his retirement plans for several years, just to help the Clinton administration. Underwood was, as they say in Washington political circles, "a very well-connected person". When he did retire, it would be with honors. Underwood would be remembered and lauded by beltway insiders long after he was gone.

Giordano had never met the Director, but he had seen photographs of the man. It was said that Underwood was unpretentious, yet a very distinguished-looking man, handsome, over six-feet tall, white hair, and clean shaven. He always dressed conservatively in dark, tailored business suits. The Director was known to be direct, professional, cunning, and extremely intelligent. When Underwood appeared, he immediately greeted Frank and asked him to come into his office. "Have a seat at the table," instructed Director Underwood. Frank complied. He was immediately impressed with the many plaques, awards, mementos, and pictures lining the walls of Underwood's immaculately adorned office. A large bookcase with neatly placed books was directly in front of him. What a career, Frank thought, as he briefly scanned the office walls. There were photos of Underwood posed with U.S. Presidents, powerful members of Congress, Supreme Court Justices, famous diplomats, and military leaders.

The conversation began with Underwood asking questions about comments Giordano had made on his application. Underwood wanted to know all about his life, including his past military service, civilian time, where he grew up, and who he hung out with. What had his parents done to earn a living? How was his home life? Frank was surprised by the intimacy of Underwood's questions. Giordano's life history was all well-documented on the application. Underwood wanted to learn more about his habits, likes, and dislikes, in addition to the documented facts.

After a while, Frank felt as if the unassuming man was conducting more than just a routine interview. It appeared to Giordano that he was being skillfully interrogated by this very cunning individual sitting across the table from him. Giordano talked – was interrogated - for more than 30 minutes, answering countless questions posed by Director Underwood. Near the end of the interview, Underwood inquired about Frank's interest in serving on the BSU team. Frank paused, and then said, "I have spent my entire career trying to capture criminals after their crimes were committed. I think it would be very rewarding to work with people who are actually catching the bad guys before they commit their next crimes. With my training, education, experience, and willingness to work hard, I think I can make a difference."

Underwood was silent for what seemed like a long time, but he finally looked directly at Frank and said, "I believe you will make a difference here too. Welcome to the BSU. Have a nice weekend. You can get started this coming Monday. Please report to me sharply at 8:00 a.m. and I will show you around the building, introduce you to the staff, and see to it that you get all the credentials you need as the newest member of the BSU team."

Giordano was extremely pleased that he was offered the job. He quickly rose, extended his hand, and shook Underwood's hand. "I'm humbled to meet you sir," he said. "Thank you for the kind words, praise, and acceptance. I'll see you Monday morning. I can hardly wait to begin working here."

"The pleasure is all mine, Frank," Underwood replied. "I'm pleased and excited to be adding you to our excellent BSU staff."

The drive back to Washington, D.C. seemed to take forever. The traffic was already beginning to get heavy, slow-moving, and clogged, even though it was only 1:00 p.m. Outside of the base, there were several fast food restaurants. Giordano decided to stop for a quick burger, fries, and a Coke. A decision he regretted 20 minutes later, because he had a pressing urge to use a restroom. *My nerves have finally gotten the better of me,* he thought; probably due to the interview with Director Underwood.

Frank stopped at the first gas station off the interstate, relieved himself, and inched his way back onto the I-95 North ramp. He could hardly wait to get back to their apartment and tell Marie that he had been given the job. Frank knew she would be ecstatic for him and ready to start house hunting. They both were tired of the expensive apartment living in the Washington, D.C. area, the extremely high cost of living, and the lack of adequate parking for their vehicles. Besides, Marie was already expressing concern that rodents were crawling all over their furniture in the storage warehouse. Giordano figured that he had at least 45 more minutes of drive time before getting back to the nation's capitol.

Once he arrived at the FBI headquarters in downtown Washington, with its massive concrete buildings and an occasional natural area filled with green grass, flowers, and trees, he was confident and ready for a new job and in a new location. Giordano planned to immediately inform his temporary boss of the transfer to Quantico scheduled for the following Monday. He would gather his personal items from his desk and head home. But before he departed, Giordano wanted to say goodbye to the agents he had worked with in counter-intelligence.

As he drove, Frank wondered how good a fit he would be for the BSU? He hoped he had all the necessary skills to get started on another meaningful career path in the

Bureau. *Will I be accepted as a worthy replacement for the vacancy created by the death of a long-time BSU agent? I guess I will find out on Monday morning.*

Giordano was replacing Special Agent James Cooper, who had been killed in a surprise shoot-out between several BSU agents and two dangerous killers. The criminals had escaped custody from a small, rural Virginia county jail.

Just before 5:00 p.m. Frank arrived at his temporary Washington, D.C. office. He talked to his provisional supervisor, said his good-byes to several friends, then packed up his personal items and left for home.

The Giordanos' apartment was tightly packed in between two other modern apartment complexes over-looking a park several streets from the Potomac River. When he arrived home, he was still feeling pleased and excited. Not surprisingly, Marie had dinner waiting for him on the stove. "Well, how did it go?" she asked.

Giordano looked at her and smiled, "I got the job. I start Monday morning." As he expected, Marie was bursting with excitement, congratulations, and ready to move.

Chapter 2

Frank prepared for his first day on the new job by getting extra sleep Sunday night and filling up the car with gasoline. Giordano wanted to make a good first-impression with the Unit. He'd taken one of his nicer suits and a long-sleeved white shirt to the dry cleaners. Marie purchased a stylish blue and yellow tie for him from an up-scale men's clothing store in Georgetown. She also made sure there was plenty of hot coffee in his mug, a full pack of cigarettes in his pocket, and a chocolate donut wrapped in a napkin.

Marie commented on how attractive Frank looked with a fresh haircut, stylish clothing, flawless complexion, and his olive-oil colored skin. Before he departed for work, Giordano took a last look at himself in the mirror. He was pleased with how professional he looked. Marie gave him a quick sendoff kiss and said, "I love you. Have a great day."

He apprehensively said, "Thanks, I hope too."

"Just relax Frank, you'll be fine, honey. They're going

to like you."

The early Monday morning drive from Washington,
D.C. back to Quantico, Virginia, was unnerving for
Giordano. He left at 6:15 a.m. to ensure that he would be
in Director Underwood's office well before 8:00. He
thought, working for the Federal Bureau of Investigation
was a big deal. Getting assigned to the Behavioral Science
Unit within the FBI was an even bigger deal. He would be
working with some of the most outstanding criminal
investigators in the world.

The BSU was established in the early 1970's. The first
unit consisted of eleven individuals. They were tasked with
investigating serial rape and homicide cases by developing
profiles on dangerous unknown criminals. This was done
in cooperation with local law enforcement agencies over
the entire country. The fundamental mission of the BSU
was to better understand criminals. Who they are? How
they think? Why they do what they do? The belief was
that, if BSU investigators could answer those questions,
they would help solve more crimes and prevent further
criminal activity from occurring. The BSU worked closely
with the National Center for the Analysis of Violent Crime
along with local police agencies.

Surprisingly, I-95 South traffic cooperated with Frank
and allowed him to arrive 40 minutes early. He breezed
through security and headed for Underwood's office. As he
entered the Director's sanctum Giordano noticed that
Underwood was sipping coffee with one hand and paging
through a ream of official-looking documents with the
other hand. Frank quietly seated himself on the couch.

After a minute, Underwood looked up, realized Frank had entered unannounced, smiled and said, "Good morning. I see you too are an early riser."

Frank nodded and smiled inwardly with satisfaction that he'd gotten off on the right foot with his new boss. He replied, "Good morning, sir. Yes, I am an early riser. I was unsure how long the commute would take me, so I allowed myself thirty minutes leeway."

"Well done, Frank. Are you ready for your tour of the building?" Underwood asked in a cordial tone.

"I can hardly wait to tour the facility!" Frank hoped he did not sound too eager, but figured enthusiasm was expected and would be appreciated by the Director.

"I'm almost ready, but I have an important call to make before I leave the office. Make yourself comfortable. The call will not take very long. My secretary will get you a cup of coffee in the meantime."

"Thank you, sir," Giordano replied appreciatively.

* * *

Around 8:00 a.m., Underwood hung up the phone and gestured for Frank to follow him out of the office for a tour of the facility. The tour started in the basement of the building where the BSU and its support staff were housed. There were several dozen people in the main office. Underwood clapped his hands for attention and announced, "This is our new man. His name is Frank

Giordano and he has been an investigator with the Bureau in various capacities for over twenty years. His full name is Francis Albert Giordano. During my interview with Frank he shared a story, which I thought you might find interesting. His mother named him after Francis Albert Sinatra, a/k/a Old Blue Eyes, the singer/actor from Hoboken, New Jersey. Giordano hails from New Jersey too and is obviously of Italian descent." Frank's hair was jet black, as were his eyes and he was shorter than the average agent. Staff members chuckled at that, but Underwood frowned and continued, "I believe Giordano has the potential to be a *real* star - like many of you - unlike Sinatra, who was connected to a Mafia Don."

Underwood allowed himself a slight smile, then turned serious again, "Ladies and gentlemen, I am relying on you to help Frank reach the highest level of performance and professionalism with all due haste. As you know, we have a large caseload to investigate and I would like it to be done sooner rather than later."

In almost perfect unison the group responded, "Yes sir, we will!"

"Good," Underwood flatly stated. He eyed each of the men and women assembled in front of him and then went on, "Incidentally, Frank was greatly involved in the recent events concerning the terrorist attacks in southwest Michigan. He spearheaded one of the two major investigations and was instrumental in helping to compile valuable information about the case. Ultimately, Frank's work culminated with the apprehension and arrest of several perpetrators. I am giving him a general tour of the facility and then I will bring him back for the indoctrination process. We are enthused that he is joining us and I know he is excited as well."

"Welcome to the BSU Frank," said a moderately tall, average-size, middle-aged man, standing near the center of the group. Giordano assumed he was in charge of the unit. "We've already heard lots of good things about you, Frank. I'll introduce you formally to all the members of the staff when you return. I'm Supervising Special Agent Gary Larcovic."

"I appreciate that," Giordano replied sincerely. Frank took in all the faces gathered in the room staring at him. He felt a little intimidated, but mostly excited at the prospect of working with this caliber of professionals.

"Mr. Larcovic will be your direct supervisor," said Underwood. "Pay close attention to him and you will learn a lot."

Giordano nodded in acknowledgement. "Thank you, sir. I will."

"Let's continue with the tour, Frank," Underwood said, as he turned and signaled Giordano to follow him.

On the first floor Underwood showed Frank the location of the personnel office. "Before you head back downstairs, stop in their office and they will provide you with all the security badges and credentials that you are going to need."

Frank was pleased and impressed that Underwood was being so generous with his time as he showed Frank the cafeteria and the various crime laboratories in the building.

The criminal computer information database was in the basement, along with the BSU staff. He also pointed out some of the other executive offices located on the second through the fifth floors. Underwood gave Frank a brief but thorough overview of the many activities conducted in the various spaces they visited.

Frank was tremendously impressed that Underwood personally conducted the tour rather than assigning the job to an underling, as many figures with his authority would. Maybe that's one of the reasons Underwood is such a successful leader, thought Giordano. He wants the new employees to feel that they are wanted, needed, and properly welcomed.

Following the tour, Frank spent the next hour in the personnel office, filling out forms and paperwork. When he returned to the basement offices, he possessed all the keys, clearances, badges, and paperwork necessary to begin work at the BSU.

Gary Larcovic was waiting for him in his office. "I'll bet you are glad to get the paperwork and clearance stuff out of the way; am I right?" Larcovic asked with a ready smile.

"Yes sir, I'm ready to go to work, Mr. Larcovic," Frank replied crisply. He noted that he was more stylishly dressed than his supervisor.

"Please, call me Gary or Boss, Frank. And there's no need for the 'sir'. We're a small, close-knit group. We work a little differently than what you might be used to in the Bureau."

"Well, alright Gary," said Frank, feeling a little uncomfortable with the informality that the brown-haired man, standing in front of him, had recommended. Larcovic was six-feet tall and displayed the necessary leadership qualities to be in command. He graduated from the University of Pennsylvania and received his Masters in Psychology at their remote campus in Pittsburgh. He had physical strength and a bad temper, if unnecessarily provoked. And, he was Croatian with a strong work ethic and resolve. Gary had grown up in the working-class neighborhood of Lawrenceville, near downtown Pittsburgh, Pennsylvania. His father worked in a foundry and his mother was a homemaker. He was recently divorced and was having a rough time of it, trying to explain to his two young children the reasons for their split. Larcovic was a patriotic and dedicated American too. He was also very conservative and generally dressed the part.

"Follow me," said Larcovic leading Giordano into a small, sparsely decorated, cream-colored room. The room had no windows, only a small round table and four chairs. Frank noticed a compact refrigerator filled with 8-ounce water bottles in the corner. "Is it alright if I take one?" Frank asked.

"Yes, that's what they're here for, Frank," Larcovic said as he closed the door behind them. "This is a secure space, so anytime we enter this room no one can hear what we are discussing from the outside. For the next few weeks, this will be your training facility."

Larcovic gestured at a chair on the near side of the round table. "Have a seat Frank and I'll begin with the indoctrination process." Larcovic looked at some papers he was holding and said, "The first subject is serial killers. I'm sure you have a general idea about them, since you've worked in the Bureau for several decades."

Frank nodded. "I do. However, I'm sure there is a lot more to learn."

Larcovic took a seat across the table from Frank. "Yes, there is, and we're going to remedy that starting today," Larcovic said dryly. So began Frank's initial tutorial.

"All serial killers have a unique affinity for power," was Larcovic's opening line. And then he dug into the topic. "They want to control people, even when they're caught. They are great at manipulation, so they can present themselves in a false light. Their ability to manipulate is their way of hiding their sinister personalities. Serial killers have been known to brag about the atrocities they've committed, whether it's to their next victims, accomplices, the police, or even to themselves. They are very talented at charming people and have a firm grasp of other people's emotions. Serial killers can quickly ascertain a person's vulnerabilities and weaknesses. They can convince their victims to do things they would normally not do. They know how to get people to lower their guards in certain circumstances."

Larcovic paused and looked at Frank meaningfully. "Ted Bundy, for instance, was described as being charming, charismatic, and handsome. He killed thirty-six known female victims, but we are sure there were more.

The scariest trait about most serial killers is their ability to pass themselves off as being normal individuals or even pillars of their communities."

Larcovic went on, "In the nomenclature of the Bureau, in order to classify someone as a serial killer, they must have killed separately at least three times. The evidence in the case should indicate that the killer felt compelled to completely dominate the victim. Most serial killers have a strong urge to commit murder, but they are typically extremely cautious in choosing their victims. They want to optimize their chances for success, because they don't want to get caught. Many times, their first victims are either prostitutes or homeless people, who would be unlikely to be missed by anyone. Once they start killing, they generally have no intention of ever stopping, unless they are either caught, killed, or die of natural causes."

Larcovic's eyes drilled into Frank's. "Another scary thing about this type of person is you could be an acquaintance of theirs for years and have no idea of what they are capable of. Some serial killers have experienced no childhood abuse, no apparent trauma, and do not possess the general characteristics associated with serial killers. The personalities and lifestyles of serial killers are complex and varied."

"Let me give you another example," Larcovic said. "Take the case of Dennis Rader, the BTK killer, from Wichita, Kansas. His wife had no idea her husband was a serial killer. Rader was the oldest of four boys. He had a seemingly common childhood with two normal parents. There were no known reports of pathologies within the family while Rader was growing up. However, it was later learned that he had killed stray animals, but had masked such disturbing behavior as a child. Generally, there will be some kind of 'tell' in a serial killer's record. It is very rare to find someone like Rader with his seemingly normal background. Incidentally, Rader killed ten people before he was arrested. On the other hand, the only explanation for some of these people is that they are just plain crazy and evil."

Larcovic had been leaning forward speaking directly and firmly at Frank across the table. His tone was not overly aggressive or angry, but it carried weight. Finally, he tilted his head back and relaxed in his chair. He glanced at his wristwatch, and then said in a more casual tone, "Frank, if you have any questions about what I've tried to impart to you in broad brush-strokes and a couple examples, feel free to ask. It's almost lunch time and we can continue with the subject in the cafeteria. But you might want a different topic of conversation with food on your plate," Larcovic said with a wry grin.

Frank returned the grin, but immediately turned serious again. "Clearly, there's a lot more I need to learn about serial killers. Can you put a number on how many unknown serial killers are active in the United States at present?"

"Nobody knows for sure, but it is conservatively estimated that there are at least two thousand - probably more. It should give you chills to imagine there are that many serial killers roaming around the country, hunting for their next victims," Larcovic said unsmiling. "Serial killers can be emotionally vacant and incapable of forming healthy relationships. Good relationships are what make us human. Serial killers do not have good relationships. They are anti-social, deceitful, and manipulative. Most of them have early behavioral problems, so they do not develop empathy for others. They are smooth but insincere talkers; they lack remorse, and any sense of guilt."

"Wow! I do have more questions, but my stomach is telling me it's definitely ready for lunch. Is it alright if we take a break in the cafeteria and resume with my questions and your answers when we return?"

"Absolutely Frank, that sounds like a good plan. I'm kind of hungry myself."

After returning to the training room, Larcovic answered a question Giordano raised concerning how to recognize serial killers. "Ninety-two percent of serial killers are men. There are a few female serial killers, but they are pretty rare. Fifty-two percent of serial killers are white males in their twenties and thirties. The average span of a serial killer's career is between two to three years. However, some get caught in one month and others go on for twenty-plus years. Some never get caught and remain anonymous for a lifetime, but that's pretty unusual. Their average IQ is an unimpressive ninety-five – which may seem surprising given how cleverly manipulative many of them are. Our research indicates that their first kill usually occurs when they are around twenty-seven years old."

Larcovic raised his eyebrows and drew his lips tight, then said, "This might surprise or disappoint you, but about twenty-five percent of all serial killers are veterans."

Frank straightened, furrowed his brow, and replied questioningly, "Really?"

"Yep, I'm afraid so. Our statistics reveal that about a quarter of serial killers served in some branch of the United States military." Larcovic leaned back in his chair and said, "This probably won't surprise you. Serial killers come from single parent households eighty-five percent of the time.

Frank nodded, "Huh."

Larcovic went on, "Forty percent of all serial killers kill for enjoyment, lust, the thrill of it, and power/control. Almost always, serial killers enjoy watching their victims suffer. Usually, serial killers torture their prey before they kill them. They derive feelings of power from torturing and killing. Serial killers are classified in two ways. The first type is based on motives, the second on organizational and social patterns. We'll discuss those things in more detail later in your indoctrination."

"Sounds good," Giordano muttered.

"Serial killers have a vision in mind to help them identify their victims," Larcovic said. "That is one way that they can be vulnerable. If our investigators can figure out who is at risk, we have a better chance of catching the perpetrators. You see," Larcovic paused for effect, "Serial killers want to feel complete control over their victims and they thrive on seeing their victims' fears displayed. To them, murder is the ultimate form of dominance over a human being. All of them experience a trigger mechanism, such as a traumatic event or a memory of abuse, which combined with other factors, can cause a dangerous, violent impulse. When they experience this trigger event or violent impulse, it will usually activate their inner desire to kill. Once they begin killing, it becomes an insatiable desire that they want to do over and over again. Sometimes, these violent impulses are repeated very quickly and in other cases they are not. It just depends on the individual's psychopathy."

"What factors contribute to the creation of most serial killers?" Giordano interjected.

"Excellent question, Frank." Larcovic nodded with approval. "Childhood abuse, mental, physical, or sexual is almost always an important factor. Most serial killers come from unstable homes. Most are psychopaths suffering from an anti-social personality disorder. They place very little value on human life. They target, stalk, assault, and kill their victims. They have no sense of remorse or sympathy for their victims."

Larcovic whet his lips and continued, "Our research indicates there are some early childhood warning signs to watch for in serial killers. It's often discovered that serial killers tortured and killed animals intentionally in their youth and committed arson. They display anti-social behavior, come from homes where drug or alcohol abuse has been present, and are bed-wetter's past the normal childhood stage. Their parent or parents usually have criminal backgrounds. There are other things to watch for, but these are the most common characteristics known to date." Larcovic grunted, rubbed the back of his neck, looked at his watch, and said, "Frank, it's almost five. Let's call it quits for today. We can resume tomorrow."

"Okay. That sounds good to me," Giordano said, and then he too rubbed the back of his neck and stretched his spine.

"If you were wondering whether your notes will be adequate, don't worry. The entire course is encapsulated in our indoctrination workbook, which you will get at the conclusion of the process."

"Great! I'm glad you told me that, Gary. I was beginning to get worried. You've given me such a boatload of information already," Giordano breathed a sigh of relief.

"Yes, it's a lot of information to grasp in such a short time. We have a sizeable caseload, so this process won't last as long as you might expect. By next week, you and I might be out in the field looking at evidence and trying to develop a profile on an unknown criminal subject, who we refer to in the BSU as an 'unsub'."

"Really, do you think I'll be ready that soon?" Giordano asked with a twinge of nervousness.

"Don't worry. We have a very good team and you'll be individually guided along the way. That is, until I feel you are ready for some independent work on your own."

Larcovic slapped the table with finality, stood up, and walked out the training room door. Frank followed him out and quickly headed for the bathroom. I need to use the facilities, before I drive home, he thought.

Chapter 3

Early Saturday morning, April 10, 2004, the day before Easter, on the south side of Montgomery, Alabama the weather was a chilly 52 degrees. It was raining and the weather conditions were expected to be miserable for the next few hours. Prostitutes were huddled next to buildings and under lighted areas where they could be easily seen and protected from the elements. The Johns were there too cruising the streets looking to pick up hookers.

In Montgomery the going price for fellatio was $40. Fornication usually cost $85, but price was always negotiable. The hooker's looks, age, race, and marketing skills upped or lowered her price, depending on the John's taste. There were always plenty of women out on the stroll, so prices remained relatively stable. The police rarely interrupted the trade in human flesh. They had more serious criminal activities to pursue. Hookers exist in high risk situations and are often involved with drug/alcohol abuse. They are the socially marginalized people in any community. If their pimps or Johns abuse them, who cares? When they go missing, who will remember them?

Society pays more attention to dead whores than to the

living ones. Their corpses may be found abandoned, decaying along rural highways, secluded river banks, in dense forests, or buried in shallow graves. The bodies are usually not immediately discovered, which makes it more difficult for investigators to determine the decedent's identification, cause, and time of death. If the detective is lucky, the forensic team can determine the victim's identity by finger print examination, that is, if the deceased had a record. Dental records and photographs of missing people can be compared to the decomposed bodies, which might get a hit for the investigators.

The driving rain stopped momentarily and the sky cleared, at least temporarily. One of the John's cruising just off I-82 was particularly interested in assessing a certain prostitute he had passed earlier on the street. She was a short, pretty, white woman, standing under a street lamp. He thought she looked very appealing and perfect for his needs. She wore tight jeans, high heels, and large, hoop ear-rings. He drove slowly toward where she stood along the street. His gaze confirmed she was young, maybe eighteen or nineteen, probably only weighed a hundred pounds soaking wet. She did not have the typical hardened look of a full-fledged prostitute. Not yet, anyway. It was obvious that she used lots of make-up and probably wore cheap perfume to be more enticing. He assumed she was relatively new to the stroll.

Earlier, she had noticed him too. He looked to be medium-sized, older, and drove a late model 1990's minivan. The man had circled the block twice before and was looking at her again. The vehicle pulled up to the curb and a muscular, average looking, casually dressed man said, "Hi there."

The hooker looked the man over for a couple of seconds. He had a dark tan, weathered facial features, medium-sized physique, average height, and looked to be in his mid-forties, a typical John out looking for sex. She responded, "Hey baby, lookin' for a date tonight?"

"Well, maybe, if the price is right."

"What do you have in mind?" she asked as she thrust out her chest and twirled a lock of bleached-blond hair.

"Head, but what do you charge for everything?" he asked evenly.

"I usually get a hundred, but I'd do it for eighty-five, because of the weather. You ain't a cop, are you?"

"No, do I look like one?" he replied with a laugh.

"No, but I always ask," she said as she opened the door and slid into the passenger seat of the minivan.

"I understand," he said. "Your price is fine. Where do you want to go?"

"About five blocks from here there's a vacant lot next to an abandoned building. We can go there."

"Okay, just point the way. Are you thirsty for something to drink? I've got water and soft drinks in the cooler behind my seat."

"Yeah, water sounds good," she said with a note of gratitude in her voice.

"There should be one left. You can help yourself. Just reach back and take the bottle out of the cooler."

While the hooker turned to reach into the cooler the man's expression changed briefly from warm and friendly to anxious. She did not notice the brief but radical change in her John. The hooker was too absorbed with anticipation of a cool drink. She grabbed the water bottle, removed the cap, and drank several big gulps.

Resuming his friendly, reassuring voice, the man offered, "There's more in my other cooler, in the back. Just let me know if you want another one."

"Thanks," she said. "You from Montgomery?" asked the prostitute in a sweet, conversational tone.

"Yeah, I live northeast, outside of the city. How much farther?"

"It's not too far now," she said as they stopped for a traffic light. "It's just a few more blocks ahead on the right."

Three blocks later, the man slowly turned the minivan into a vacant lot and drove up close to the abandoned building the whore pointed to. He stopped, shifted into park, and said, "Let's go behind the front seat and lay down there. All the seats have been removed and it's carpeted. It'll be more comfortable."

"Sure, whatever you want, honey" she said smiling.

"Take your time," said the man. "Finish the drink and afterwards, I'll get you a fresh one."

"Okay," she said. "But I need the eighty-five up-front."

"If you're really good, I could be persuaded to give you the full hundred dollars," he said. "Oh hell, I know you're going to be good." He pulled out a wallet from his back pocket and handed her a crisp $100 bill.

They climbed into the back and she immediately began to remove his clothing and kiss his semi-naked body. With some relief she thought, *this won't take as long as if we were fumbling around in the front seat.* With the Ben Franklin tucked securely in her jeans pocket she decided this would be her last trick for the night. The thought of taking a hot shower and getting out of her wet clothes increased the speed at which she was working to get this guy off.

"Let's take it a little slower, sweetheart," he said. I want this to be very memorable."

"Okay, if that's what you want." She slowed her pace and began to tease him removing her jeans and panties in a provocative way. She unbuttoned her blouse and exposed her breasts."

"No bra. Very nice," he said with obvious arousal in his voice.

"Are you a breast man?" she asked. "How do you like my rose?" She pointed to the red-rose tattoo with 'Love' on her right breast.

"I like it all," he said as he awkwardly began to explore her naked body with his hands.

At that moment, she began to slowly feel herself losing consciousness. "Hey, I feel strange. What's going on, asshole?" She grabbed his arm and tried to regain her balance.

He clutched her arms and said, "I gave you something to help you relax while I have sex with you. When you wake up in a few hours we can do even more things. Don't worry. I want this to be a very special day for you as well as me."

"What the fuck! You pervert! If you hurt me, my pimp is gonna kill you."

"Oh, I don't think so," he said calmly still holding her arms. "However, I am going to torture and kill you myself. That's how I really get off," he said with a twisted smile.

She was beginning to feel the full effect of the drug she had ingested. His words were only partially audible as she slipped under the influence of the drug. Her mind wandered in several directions. *Is he really going to torture and kill me?* In a bewildering state of semi-consciousness, she could feel the weight of his body and the usual rhythmic thrusting on top of her. There was a flicker of anger knowing she was being raped and this was ... she entered a state of deep sleep.

* * *

When she awoke, hours later, she was confused. At first, she did not know where she was. She had no recollection of what happened to her. She could feel her hands and legs were bound with tape. There was something in her throat blocking her ability to scream or talk. She was totally naked and was lying on a carpeted floor. She realized she was in a moving vehicle when she felt motion and the noise of an automobile being driven somewhere. Some kind of a tarp covered her. No one would be able to see her naked body through the car windows. She could barely breathe. The tarp had a stale odor and made her itch where it touched her naked body. There was a disgusting substance which had dried onto the fabric of the tarp. She tried to scream, but could not. Her face and eyes were covered with a mask, so she could not see. Her vagina was extremely sore.

"I see from your movement that you are awake," said the voice of a man. "Did you sleep well? You missed a remarkable morning," he said. "I took some memorable photos. By the way, don't worry, I always wear a condom when I have sex. I do this for multiple reasons, which I won't go into right now." *I always prefer a docile female instead of one who I have to fight with in order to have sex,* he thought.

She thrashed her head around and blinked rapidly trying to see through the mask while he spoke. She couldn't speak, but her mouth contorted with rage. If it wasn't for the mask, the look on her face would have told him she wanted to kill him.

After a pause to watch her ineffective squirming, he continued speaking, "You underestimate yourself. Sex with you was well worth one-hundred dollars. Too bad we couldn't have enjoyed it more together."

She tried to scream, "Go fuck yourself!" but only gurgling sounds escaped.

"I'm looking for a good place to stop and continue the

activities that I have planned for us," he said. "Unfortunately for you though, I think you might find this next phase much more uncomfortable. Still, I want us to experience it together. I'm sure you will welcome the end more readily," he said. "You see, torture is a good teaching method if properly done. Suffering needs to be introduced at a gradual pace in order for it to be truly effective. But we both know you wouldn't cooperate and behave as you should. So, we'll just have to see if torture will teach you to behave. It probably won't, but we'll see. Ultimately, you will be begging, maybe pleading with me to end your life. I know you'll never allow me to control you, no matter how severe the punishment."

He smiled to himself ruefully, shook his head, and then continued with his monologue. "You know, my mother always told me that increasing the severity of the punishment was the way to learn and I learned that lesson well. Once I understood, I always listened to her and tried to obey. I did not want her to get angry. I truly wanted to be good and earn her approval."

The woman began thrashing violently again, rolling back and forth under the cover. That there would be no opportunity to escape, plead her case, or beg for mercy had sunk in. She realized his twisted mind was already made up. He was going to kill her.

It seemed like an hour had passed when the minivan finally came to a stop and then quickly backed up. She had no idea where she was. She heard the sound of the sliding door behind the driver's seat and then felt the man's fingers grasping her feet and pulling her body out the door.

She felt dew-covered grass on her naked backside.

"We're here," he said as he removed the mask that covered her face and eyes. She squinted into bright sunlight. How long had they been traveling? Where were they? How could she escape, she desperately wondered?

He opened the back door of the minivan and retrieved a large pair of pliers, a hunting knife, a small sledge hammer, a small plastic bottle labeled "Acid-Highly Caustic", a pair of heavy-duty plastic gloves, a bottle of water, and a hand towel. He placed the items in a 5-gallon bucket, which he set down next to her.

Her face contorted in horror when she saw the items he had assembled. The look in his eyes was a mixture of abject fear and savage rage. Her struggle against the bonds finally ceased and she began to sob.

"Don't cry," he said in a tone of false concern. "It will all be over very soon." He picked her up with strong arms and slung her over his shoulder. He walked with his burden into a heavily wooded area, a fair distance from where his vehicle was parked.

He had scouted the location before. They had driven down an old logging road in the middle of nowhere. The surrounding woods should be just across the state line from Arkansas, but still in southern Mississippi, he thought. He had not seen anyone or any vehicle for the fifteen minutes he had been driving on this dirt road. He had pulled off to the side of the road, backed into a small, narrow lane, and locked the doors. The minivan was covered by low hanging pine tree limbs and branches. It was barely visible.

He was confident that, if anyone did see the vehicle, they would think it belonged to a hunter out in the woods.

"The fun is about to begin," he said with a sick gleam in his eyes. He laid her down on top of the moist pine needles, fallen branches, and brush, in a clearing inside the woods. He briefly left the clearing to retrieve his tools. When he returned, he was wearing a throw-away plastic covering. He looked like a doctor prepared for surgery. When she saw him, the woman tried to scream as loud as she could, but to no avail. She began to moan and weep again.

Prior to starting his work, the killer momentarily stopped to survey the sheltered clearing inside the vast pine woods. He listened for sounds of life and watched for the slightest movement. Neither seeing nor hearing anything of concern, the man was pleased with his choice of the secluded, quiet place. It was ideal for his purposes. He looked down at his victim and said with a twisted smile, "It's going to get pretty messy around here. Okay, let's get started, sweetheart. I'm ready when you are."

He grabbed one of her hands and pulled out a finger nail with the pliers. She screamed, but the blockage in her throat muffled the sound. "Oh, was that painful?" he asked. "Wait until I remove one of your toenails, if you think that hurt. I've been told it is more painful than removing a finger nail. Am I right?" he asked as he grabbed a foot and removed her big toenail with the pliers.

She couldn't scream or talk. She wrenched her body in pain as the nail was being extracted. She nodded helplessly acknowledging she was in severe pain. She pitifully hoped that somehow agreeing with him might earn his sympathy. She clung to the thought that cooperating with him might persuade him to spare her life. *Maybe after raping me, he is just trying to scare me into never talking? Maybe he is not going to kill me after all. I'll be his sex slave, if that will save me.*

He picked up the pliers, grasped one of her nipples and began pulling it upward. The nipple began to tear away from her breast. The nipple and the skin around it were inflamed and bleeding profusely. The pain was unbearable. He grabbed the other nipple and repeated the same procedure. She was on the verge of passing out.

After waiting a minute or so, he stopped to admire his handy work. She had experienced excruciating pain and he knew it. He felt powerful and invincible as he looked down at her wounded body. The sight of her reminded him of a stray, medium-size, female dog he had taken in and cared for, but then killed, when he was a child. Her agonized thrashing and flowing tears brought a sadistic smile to his face. The sight of the open wounds he had inflicted on her exhilarated him.

All of a sudden with one swift movement he picked up the sledge hammer and slammed it down on her right knee cap. She howled in pain, but again the sound came out as a trembling hiss. Her knee cap was shattered. Below the knee, her leg looked like it was only being held together by her skin. He slammed the hammer against her other knee and achieved the same result. She passed out. And so, it ends, he thought mercilessly.

The man picked up the large hunting knife and

methodically stabbed her multiple times in the chest. When the blade first pierced her heart, blood gushed out of the wound. When the blade penetrated a lung, even though lifeless, her body let out wheezing noises. He calmly put on the gloves, removed the cap from the bottle of acid and carefully poured the highly caustic substance all over her hands and face. He watched with fascination as the acid began to do its work. He clucked his tongue with satisfaction. There would be no fingers to print or a face to recognize. He opened her mouth, removed the cloth, and poured an extra amount of acid on her teeth. That should take care of identification by dental records.

Softly, he began to hum the melody to Bobby Darin's classic hit, *Mack the Knife*, as he admired his artistry on her torn and lifeless body. He was pleased with his work. The memory of torturing and killing her would be enough to appease his insatiable desire, until the next time.

He concealed what was left of her body under decayed grass, leaves, brush, and small pine tree branches. It would be almost impossible to identify her remains and determine much about her, other than that she had been brutally raped, tortured, and stabbed to death. He had some confidence that her identity and where she was from would not be learned from her remains. He knew, of course, that the authorities could use samples of her DNA to try to identify her. But would they even bother? And, her DNA had to be in the official database for the authorities to find the match. Did she have a record? Maybe, but she was young, so maybe not.

The killer carefully removed the plastic shroud he'd

worn to protect his clothing from blood spray during the gruesome work. He put the shroud in a black, plastic trash bag. Then, he wiped the blood and gore from his knife with the cloth he had used to stifle her screams. He poured some water out of a bottle onto his hands and washed them thoroughly and then his face. Opening up the trash bag again, he shoved the gloves, bottle, cloth, and towel inside the bag. He picked up his tools and returned to his vehicle. After he had driven several miles away from the woods, he felt satisfied and relieved. *She is my thirty-sixth victim,* he thought. *And, I have never been captured or even questioned by the authorities.* He was excited. Yet, he thought he was probably done killing. Well, at least for three or four months. He reminded himself that his annual trek back to Arkansas had afforded him this opportunity.

His thoughts drifted back to his first kill. It occurred several years before he started routinely driving back and forth to his childhood home. He killed a slutty female hitchhiker by strangulation in the front seat of his vehicle near the Florida panhandle on April 20, 1990. He remembered it vividly.

Once he realized killing loose women was the true passion of his life, he decided it would be wise to limit his kills to three or four times a year. The only mementos he saved to remember his victims were in a small scrapbook filled with photographs of the women. They were before and after shots. The book was hidden in the concealed bottom of an end-table within the table's base. The end-table was positioned next to the couch in his Florida living room. He never kept tokens like strands of hair, bones, and articles of clothing or jewelry as reminders of his conquests. The photographs were quite enough to trigger exciting memories.

Over the years, he had modified his original operating methods several times on how to select, capture, and kill his victims. He religiously read newspaper, magazine, and criminal digest accounts about serial killers. He had also seen many televised documentaries on American serial killers. The country seemed to be obsessed with crime and killing. *Cool! But they will never catch me*, he thought to himself. So far, he was correct.

The only thing that really concerned him was the possibility that he would not always be able to control his victims. Once, a very hardened and tough, older whore had briefly escaped his grasp. He found her fairly quickly, but feared that someone might have seen the disheveled woman and called the authorities. He felt compelled to kill her immediately. He regretted being unable to perform his usual ritual on her. He intended never to repeat that scenario again. It had been way too dangerous. Following that experience, he understood the importance of victim selection. It had been years since that incident. He had learned from the mistake.

Bright lights from a large, truck-stop sign attracted his attention. He was tired. It had been a long day and he was still far from home. After disposing of the trash bag in a large, commercial trash bin at the back of the truck stop, he decided to fill up his gasoline tank, eat, relieve himself, and lie down for a short nap.

As he drifted off to sleep in the back of the minivan, the memory of the cute, young, white prostitute he had tortured and killed was still pleasantly on his mind. This will be one of the more memorable kills, he thought. *I was free to spend more than an adequate amount of time with this latest victim. Usually, I am forced to kill my victims quickly, either in their motel rooms or occasionally in their homes, which doesn't allow much time for spontaneity, appreciation, and enjoyment.*

Chapter 4

Several hours before sunrise, Michael James Smith awoke, opened the sliding door to his minivan, and got out. He was stiff and sore after sleeping longer than he had planned. He stretched and slowly began to feel better. He hoped it would be another warm day. The drive to Higden, Arkansas, would probably take over four hours, depending on traffic and road construction projects.

Before he stopped to sleep in the van, Smith had made a discovery which briefly infuriated him. He had spotted a road sign indicating that he was in Arkansas. He thought he was in Mississippi when he killed the young prostitute. He intended to commit the crime in Mississippi and leave his latest victim in that state. The prior year he left a victim in an adjacent county in Arkansas, not far from where he left the current one. The error worried him. He didn't want to make it easier for the authorities to figure out the two homicides were related. He must have gotten confused by a construction detour in Mississippi. He had not been familiar with the particular area of the logging road and woods. *Damn it!* But there was nothing he could do about it now.

He had stopped for the night at a truck stop on State Road 65, just outside of Lake Village, Arkansas. The drive to Little Rock, Arkansas, he calculated, was going to be two to two and one-half hours. SR-65 started out as a two-lane road, but became a four-lane highway as it approached the Arkansas capitol. Smith planned to stop in Little Rock for an early breakfast at a long-established roadside diner. It was nothing fancy, but all the meals were tasty and home-cooked. He especially loved their biscuits with sausage gravy.

When he sat down at the counter in the Capitol City Diner, a petite, young waitress immediately came over to take his order. "Coffee, sir?"

"Yes, thank you," he said with an engaging smile. She was pretty, innocent, and returned his warm greeting. He noted her shapely figure with pleasure. *Maybe some time*, he thought to himself. But he quickly reconsidered and acknowledged that she was not actually his type.

A few minutes later, she returned, refilled his coffee cup and asked, "Ready to order?"

"Yeah, I'd like two eggs over medium, bacon, and biscuits with sausage gravy. I'd like to have some extra gravy on the side too, please."

"Sure, no problem. We'll have that out in a jiffy. We're never very busy before church services on Easter Sunday."

"Well, Happy Easter!" Smith replied, but with a shade of surprise in his tone.

"Happy Easter to you too, sir."

Smith realized the surprised enthusiasm in his reply revealed he wasn't a regular church goer. But, so what; he wasn't there to make an impression.

In less than five minutes the pretty, young waitress returned with his food. "Everything look good?" she asked as she carefully placed the warm plate of food in front of him.

"Yes, everything looks good including the help," he cracked as he slyly admired her body.

"Thank you," she said meekly and turned quickly away.

He immediately realized his comment embarrassed her, but she was trying to act as though it had not. She was probably very religious, he thought. *Maybe I'll give her a generous tip to appease her.* Still, she needs to learn that waitresses have to put up with cracks like that, especially when you're an attractive, young woman. Most men like her type. In a way, she reminded him of his sister, so young and innocent. He decided to give the waitress a break and not tease her anymore. *She's still young, but in a couple of years she will have to figure things out and not be so naïve.*

When Smith finished eating and stood up to leave, he smiled at her again. "I'll see you soon," he said, lowering his ball cap and nodding it in her direction.

"Bye," she said coldly.

Smith got into his minivan and pondered the drive for a moment. *It's probably going to take me another two hours before I'll get to Higden, Arkansas. I can hardly wait to get there. Maybe take a nap, go to the grocery store, and have an early dinner.* He was very tired. Except for his stops in

Montgomery to pick up the prostitute and then in the woods to kill her before sleeping in the minivan, he had been on the road since leaving his home in St. James City, Florida, located on the Gulf of Mexico. Breakfast at the restaurant in Little Rock was a refreshing break, but now he would push on to his house in Higden, Arkansas. *Thankfully, the remaining trip to my Higden home is almost over.*

It was mid-April. Normally, he did not leave Florida until early May. However, he had a big project to get started on at his vacation home in Higden. Besides, his hunger for the next kill had become almost unbearable, while he was in Florida. Generally, he liked to perform his killings outside the Sunshine State. In fact, his victims were scattered all over the southern United States in Louisiana, Tennessee, Mississippi, Alabama, Texas, and Georgia. Smith had also left bodies in Missouri and one in Kentucky.

It was in the early 1990's when Smith began returning annually, in the summer, to his hometown. Higden was like any of the small, seemingly forgotten towns scattered throughout the United States. There was nothing exceptional about the Higden community. It was located in upper Arkansas, nestled in the foothills of the Ozark Mountains. Many of the original residents of Higden traveled from Benton County, Tennessee on wagon trains in the late 1880's. The town is located in Cleburne County and was named after one of its founders, Thomas Geoffrey Higdon, who hailed originally from North Carolina. For some reason, the name of the town is spelled Higden instead of Higdon. Smith had asked around, but no one knew the reason for the difference in spelling. In 1959 Higden was still located in the valley, but due to flooding, it was relocated to higher ground. The town's population had declined, but it clung to life and still maintained its charter and post office.

Smith was born in 1958 in his family's home. In those years, pregnant women in Higden rarely went to a hospital to give birth. He was told that a mid-wife was summoned to assist with his delivery. A year later raging flood waters forced the family to move.

Higden encompasses about one half of a square mile, is 95 percent white and has a population of about one hundred. Early in the 1900's the population was over 300. Smith's family home has been under water in the Greer's Ferry Lake, since 1962.

For years, the Little Red River flowed through Higden without flooding. But it eventually started spilling over its banks with some frequency. Coping with the regular flooding was increasingly challenging for the residents of the small, river-valley community. Higden residents were eventually forced either to leave town or move to the new Higden located on higher ground.

In the 1950's, a dam was proposed. The construction project was recommended, approved, and undertaken by the United States Army Corps of Engineers in cooperation with the state of Arkansas. It was hoped that the dam would alleviate the flooding problem and lead to commercial development in the area. The dam was dedicated on October 3, 1963 by President John F. Kennedy. Locals claim it was the last official act of his presidency, prior to his assassination in Dallas, Texas. The dam was named after William V. Greer, who ran a ferry across the river in the 1880's.

Upon the completion of the Greer's Ferry Lake Dam, the Little Red River ceased flooding the valley. Greer's Ferry Lake was created by damming the river. The lake became one of the most popular fishing and recreational areas in the state. Today, the Little Red River is one of the blue-ribbon trout streams in America. Each year over a million rainbow trout spawns are harvested at the National Fish Hatchery in Heber Springs, Arkansas. The lake has 40,745 acres of water and is one of the cleanest and clearest lakes in the entire country with 276 miles of shoreline.

Higden's population declined to the low 40's prior to the dam's completion. The 2000 census listed the population at 101 with 34 families residing in Higden in 52 households. The surrounding area within Cleburne County is slowly making a comeback. The community is comprised of hard-working, God-fearing people, mostly blue collar and white. Approximately 20 percent of the population is living at or under the poverty level.

There are very few retail establishments in Higden. There is a Marina and a few businesses dependent on fishing and boating. Most of the locals, shop in the neighboring town of Heber Springs, about a half-hour drive to the southeast.

Each year the residents in the community sponsor a special weekend ceremony, starting with Homecoming Day on the first Saturday after Mother's Day. On Sunday, the Decoration Day ceremony commemorates the founders of Higden and their living descendants. Smith always liked to attend both events. Occasionally, a cousin or two would show up for the weekend. They'd jaw about their families, eat, and have a convivial day. On Sunday, many of the residents go out to the old Higden Cemetery, just outside of town, and put flowers on the founders' graves and on their own family graves.

Smith had no memory of the old town of Higden. Several relatives, who never left the area, have supplied details for him about old Higden. Now, most of his relatives are either dead or moved away.

Smith has a few fond memories of West Side Elementary and West Side High School where he attended classes. Smith didn't graduate from high school, but he eventually got a GED. He knew that his teachers told his mother that his intellectual capabilities were above average; although, that did not actually square with the scores on his IQ tests. His problems in school were always categorized as "behavioral problems" by the teachers and principals.

When he ran away from Higden, his court-appointed foster parents, and alcoholic mother, he planned never to return to that God-forsaken, little town. He hitch-hiked for several days ending up in central Florida.

Smith was uneducated, unskilled, and had personality issues. Still, he managed to survive using false identification documents to conceal his true identity and age, until he turned 21. Eventually, he got a job in a mobile-home factory where he learned basic electrical, plumbing, and general construction skills. The job lasted for several years, but he got fired for insubordination and harassing other employees. His personality problems kept him from holding any job for very long. But he had an aptitude for construction work and managed to hold onto an apprenticeship with a home builder in south Florida long enough to learn the trade. After several years, he decided to become a private contractor, so he would not have to put up with other people's shit, as he told anyone willing to listen. He established "Michael's Handy Man Services" and gradually developed a steady pipeline of customers.

The work was relatively easy and he could set his own schedule and prices. Smith enjoyed working alone and, for all appearances, seemed to be satisfied with his life. But thoughts and memories of how harshly his mother had treated him, and had repeatedly made fun of him when he was a teenager, gnawed at his consciousness. At times it caused him unbearable, but undirected anger. He had started to hate his mother when he was a child for her abusiveness, and she knew it. Unhealthy feelings of distress and rage started developing during his childhood and increased through adolescence.

Watching his mother bring her so called "boyfriends" back to their house, after disappearing for several hours, disgusted him. When she reappeared, she was usually in a drunken stupor. He thought she was a drunken whore and he regretted ever being born by her. She blamed him for everything and routinely took out her frustrations on him, viciously beating and abusing him. Smith hated her, but he also hated hearing kids in school talk about the town whore, his mother. By the time he was twelve, he began to seriously think about killing her. The one bright spot in life was his younger sister. He protected her, and provoked his mother into beating him rather than his little sister.

Emily Ann was taken from the family after his mother was arrested for prostitution. Family services obtained a court order for Emily Ann to be placed in a foster home. After one year, the order was made permanent by the court. Her foster parents adopted Emily Ann. Smith had not seen or heard from his sister in years. He had no idea where she was living or what happened to her. Emily Ann was lost to him and he felt sad whenever he thought about her. While he did not even know if she was still alive, one thought pleased him – she had escaped their mother's tyrannical abuse. Smith hoped his sister was happy. Something that did make him happy, whenever he thought about it, was that his mother had been murdered in 1980. The case was never solved.

By the time he pulled into his freshly laid stone driveway on the outskirts of Higden, he was exhausted. Smith was drained from the trip physically, but he also was mentally distraught from remembering and reminding himself of his unfortunate past. He blamed his mother for all the difficulties in his life.

After he unloaded the Dodge minivan, he hurried inside the newly built log cabin and sat down in his favorite easy chair. He pulled out two graphic Polaroid photos of his latest victim and smiled. Smith felt the kindling urge for the next one even though his last was a very satisfying kill.

Chapter 5

On Monday morning at 9:14 a.m. Giordano was in the office starting his third week of training at the BSU. Gary Larcovic, Frank's supervisor, was describing the most advanced protocols the BSU had developed on serial killers. The conference door opened and Sarah Coughlin, Larcovic's secretary, stuck her head inside and said, "Excuse me Mr. Larcovic, there's an urgent call for you. It's Director Underwood."

"I better take that call," he said smiling at his secretary. Before leaving the room, he turned to Frank and said, "I'll be right back. You can finish reading the material while I'm gone."

Larcovic entered his office, closed the door, and picked up the telephone receiver. "Larcovic speaking, Director Underwood. What can I do for you, sir?"

"Gary, I just got a call from an aide to Karl Rove, President George W. Bush's Political Adviser and Chief of Staff. Rove is requesting our assistance in investigating a female murder victim recently found in a southern Arkansas forest. Governor Huckabee called the President and asked for help to take care of the matter expeditiously. Huckabee is seriously thinking about running for the Presidency in the next election. He doesn't want people to think he allows heinous murders to occur rampantly in Arkansas. Incidentally, this is the second victim found in two years in the southernmost part of the State. Last year, there was a murder in Ashley County. This one is in Chicot County. Both counties are right next to each other."

"Doesn't sound like a coincidence, does it," Larcovic said rhetorically.

"No, it doesn't," Underwood replied. Also, according to Rove's aide, the Sheriff in Ashley County talked with Sheriff Cecil White of Chicot County and they determined that the descriptions of the victims' conditions were similar. I'd like you to take one of your teams down there and look into the case immediately. I don't know if we are dealing with a serial killer or not, but it sounds like a real possibility. Between you and me, I owe Huckabee a huge favor and I'd like to help him out," Underwood said pointedly.

"I'll get a team together and we'll be there this afternoon. I'm training our new recruit, Giordano, and we both need a break. It will be good for him to see how we operate in the field."

"Thank you, Gary. I appreciate it."

"No problem, Director, I'm happy to help you out." Seconds later, Larcovic called Sarah Coughlin. "Sarah, we are heading to Arkansas this afternoon to investigate a murder case. Please, arrange for a plane and notify

Anthony, Roger, and either Peter or James in forensics, whoever is available. Tell them to get ready for an assignment. I don't know how long we'll be gone, but it could be several days. Further, let them know I plan to conduct a briefing in the conference room as soon as possible. We will leave at 11:00 a.m. Director Underwood will provide the case file. I want a copy for everyone on the team, so we can get up to speed before we arrive in Arkansas."

"I'll get right on it, Boss."

Larcovic appreciated the urgent tone in her voice. "Also, I'd like you to call the Sheriff's office in Chicot County. Tell them we are coming and ask them to have someone meet us at the Chicot County Airport. We should be there around 2:00 p.m. this afternoon."

"Will there be anything else?"

"No, I don't think so." Larcovic hoped he had remembered everything he needed from his secretary prior to the departure for Arkansas.

Giordano was still reading when Larcovic reappeared. "Better call your wife, Frank, and tell her you won't be home for several days. Get your travel bag and meet me in the conference room for a briefing in 30 minutes."

"What's going on, Gary?"

"We are headed for Arkansas to investigate a murder. This will be a good experience for you, Frank. I'll tell you more at the briefing." Larcovic hurried out the door.

Giordano headed for the locker/storage area and

retrieved his travel suitcase. The case contained enough clothing for up to 3 days. He called Marie to tell her the news. She was happy for him, but disappointed she would have to postpone her appointment with the realtor. Marie and Frank intended to buy a home close to his work in Quantico. Their realtor had recommended the communities of Aquia Harbor, Montclair, and Stafford, Virginia, based on housing affordability, convenience to his job, and the caliber of people living in the area. After Marie ended the call from Frank, she called the realtor and cancelled their appointment.

In the conference room, staff members started to arrive with briefcases, suitcases, and equipment for the trip. Anthony Rodriguez was first to arrive. Rodriquez was originally from the Dallas, Texas area. He was a graduate of the University of Texas in Austin. Prior to joining the BSU, Rodriguez was a renowned FBI investigator. His career in law enforcement started with the Texas Rangers. He was broad-shouldered and six-feet tall with black hair and a wind-burned face revealing noticeable scars on both cheeks. Rodriguez was of Mexican decent. His family moved to the United States when Anthony was a small child. They emigrated from Monterrey, Mexico. The family came seeking job opportunities in Texas. Anthony Rodriguez grew up in a family that was extremely poor and struggled to put food on the table. But Anthony didn't resent the struggles. He developed a strong work ethic and was a really tough guy. To his colleagues, he was one of the nicest, easy going men they knew. Anthony was married and had three small children. His voice had an unmistakable Texas drawl tinged with a Spanish accent, which greeted Larcovic and Giordano as Rodriguez entered the room.

The next to arrive was Roger Bouldon, who was originally from the New Orleans area. He was a descendant of the Creole colonial-aristocracy. Bernard Marigny was an ancestor. Marigny was a gambler, duelist, and playboy, as well as one of the guiding forces in developing New Orleans into a great American city. Bouldon was forty-years old and wealthy. He joined the BSU right out of college and was closing in on completing two decades within the department. His subordinates claimed that he possessed a sixth sense of intuitive powers and skills. Bouldon, on the other hand, claimed his "sixth sense" was actually a spiritual connection. Bouldon was an absolute genius. He was a graduate of Tulane University in downtown New Orleans and earned his Master's Degree from Yale. He was credited individually for solving several serial murder cases. Roger was not well-liked by most of his colleagues. At times, he was temperamental, conceited, impatient, and rude. And, he was a lady's man. Women were quite willing to overlook his unattractive personality traits, because of his striking good looks. He was white, single, over six-feet tall, muscular with curly blond hair, and riveting blue eyes. Bouldon always dressed casually, vigorously worked out at the gym, and had a line of bullshit most women couldn't resist.

Peter Sloan was a medical doctor, a forensics expert, single, and at 34-years of age was the youngest member of the team. Sloan was also a tech genius. No one in the BSU could match his experience and skill in the use of technical devices and computers. Sloan was smaller than Giordano at five feet, six inches tall. He wore horn-rimmed glasses, had brown hair and eyes, a pale complexion and a slight build. He looked like a weakling. The team doubted he could punch his way out of a paper bag. His excessively polite manners enhanced his wimpy reputation. Yet, he was always willing to help any team member with a tech issue, whether professional or personal. Sloan was originally from Chicago, where he attended Northwestern University and studied at the world-renowned Feinberg School of Medicine. His father was a famed bio-medical scientist, who owned more than a dozen patents. One of the most famous cases Peter Sloan helped to solve was the Green River Killer case. Gary Ridgway, the perpetrator, was convicted of murdering 48 separate individuals. Sloan quietly entered the room. With a studied look on his face he picked up one of the copies of the case file. He adjusted his glasses and began reading through the documents while still standing. He didn't speak a word to anyone in the room.

Larcovic rose and instructed the agents to take a seat and passed copies of the case file to the other agents. Each file contained photographs of the victim, a description of the victim's wounds, a map of the general crime area, and a description and pictures of the crime scene. Identification documents of the person who found the body were also in the file. The Chicot County Sheriff's department had compiled the information. It was all standard; there was nothing exceptional about the file, as far as serial murder cases go. "The local Coroner opined that the body was in the forest, for approximately a week before it was found," Larcovic pointed out. "Unfortunately, it had rained for two days prior to the discovery of the body. Your thoughts, gentlemen?"

Sloan was the first to speak. "Between the Sheriff Department's staff report, the Coroner, the person who found the body, and in spite of the rain, there might be enough evidence to glean some interesting facts about the perp. There might still be tire marks at the scene. However, we presumably have no witnesses to the crime and the police report states that all of the victim's fingerprints and her facial features, including her teeth, were mutilated beyond recognition. That's going to make an ID challenging." Sloan sighed, "This one isn't going to be easy to solve."

"Well," Larcovic replied glumly, "When the Chief of Staff to the President of the United States calls and asks for assistance, we are going to do our best to solve the case. I'm sure you all agree."

There was a murmuring of assent from the assembled group.

Larcovic was pleased with the look of serious resolve he saw on each face of the members of his team.

"We take off in thirty minutes, men. Oh, another thing, I wanted to let you know that Giordano is joining us. Use him as much as you can. After all, he is a very experienced investigator and a twenty-year agent. Any more comments or questions?"

Rodriguez spoke up, "This guy looks like he must be a real sick-o. We need to do everything we can to get him off the streets."

Bouldon nodded, but there was a touch of sarcasm in his reply. "You are absolutely correct this time, Rodriguez." Bouldon had a habit of pointing out the foibles and errors of anyone he worked with. He had caught Rodriguez in an error on one of their other current cases. So, he enjoyed riding him whenever the chance arose. But no one was smiling. His fellow agents knew Bouldon was a perfectionist, and, on occasion, could be a real asshole too. Sensing he had made a mistake by bringing it up, Bouldon quickly back-peddled and said, "Our unsub must have had a lot of fun torturing the poor girl. I wonder how long she lasted until he killed her?" With his slow, easily recognizable Louisiana/Creole accent, he added, "I'll bet not too long, judging from her injuries."

"Hopefully, we will find that out and more," Larcovic said as his eyes bore into Bouldon's.

Bouldon knew what that stare meant. He gulped and looked away knowing it would be unwise to make another comment.

"Let's gather our things and be ready to leave," Larcovic said abruptly and stood up. "The van is almost here to take us to our plane. I asked Sheriff White to have someone pick us up at the Chicot County Airport at 2:00 p.m. I don't intend to be late," Larcovic concluded in an irritated and officious tone.

Chapter 6

The plane circled the small field at the Chicot County Airport and made its final approach to the runway ten minutes ahead of schedule. Larcovic stirred nervously in his seat anticipating the landing. He hoped the runway was large enough to land the jet. He was anxious to get to work on the ground. The BSU team had flown to Arkansas, very comfortably, in an 8-passenger, 2000 model, Citation jet. Larcovic was grateful for the speed and convenience of air travel, but he hated to fly. He hoped his flying phobia was unknown to the team of experienced investigators. That was, of course, a foolish wish, given that his team was made up of professionals who made their living observing people. His underlings never teased him about flying, but it was their private joke.

The airplane was a small Citation jet leased by the Federal government for the BSU. An attractive stewardess appeared and announced their arrival just prior to landing. After the landing, the plane taxied toward a nearby hanger. When the engines were shut down, the stewardess opened the jet's cabin door, activated the mechanical ladder, and helped the passengers disembark. A lone airport employee appeared with a luggage cart and opened the exterior compartments on the plane and removed the group's luggage.

A large, white passenger van with a Chicot County emblem driven by a tall, thin, law enforcement officer pulled up at the hanger. The officer identified himself as Chicot County Deputy Sheriff Charlie Pickering. "Glad to have you boys here," Pickering said. His voice was calm, but he eyed the group of agents nervously.

"We're very glad to be here," Larcovic replied.

"After finding the deceased woman's body late yesterday afternoon and the pressure being put on us by Governor Huckabee's staff to resolve this case, well, we really have a mess on our hands," Officer Pickering said with an anxious note in his voice.

"I understand the urgency of the situation, and hopefully, we will be able to get our phase of the investigation completed quickly," Larcovic replied, trying to instill some confidence in the Deputy Sheriff. *"Yes, I got a call too, but from the White House staff,"* Larcovic thought, but didn't say it.

"The Sheriff hopes so too," Pickering said. "I'm supposed to take y'all out to the woods where the body was found. Sheriff White will meet you there. We've also arranged for you to interview the fella who found the body."

"Sounds good," Larcovic replied curtly.

"Y'all can get in the van while we load her up with y'alls luggage and equipment."

After the van was on the road Pickering said, "The person who reported finding the body was a hunter. His eight-year old son was with him and saw the corpse too. The poor kid's probably gonna need therapy after seeing her mangled remains. It's a shame. Those folks are good, God-fearing people. The crime scene was quite a shock to them. Harry Boyd - the feller who found the body - and his family live about eight minutes from where the corpse was discovered. I go to church with them. They're friends of mine," he said shaking his head sadly.

"We are anxious to meet Mr. Boyd. How far are we from where the body was located?" asked Larcovic.

"She was found in the southeastern most corner of Chicot County. If you didn't know the territory, you might easily believe you were still in Mississippi," Pickering noted with a sly smile, "but you're not. It'll take about fifteen minutes to get there from here."

As they approached the turn off to the crime scene, Pickering said, "We'll turn right on the next dirt road. This area used to be good farm and logging land, until the Mississippi River started routinely flowing over its banks. Now, it's mostly used by utility workers, hunters, and kids coming out here to park at night. Sometimes you can see the flooded terrain and the water line. The water has come as close as a quarter mile from here. Just depends on the amount of rain and melted snow that runs into the river from upstream."

"We were told it's been raining here for the past several days," Larcovic said.

"Yep, it rained here alright, but not too hard. The

wind's been pickin' up though." The nervous tone returned to Pickering's voice. "I hope it won't hinder your investigation any."

"We'll do what we can in spite of the rain and wind conditions." Larcovic turned and looked back at Bouldon and said, "I hope someone is taking notes on the Deputy Sheriff's comments."

"Yes, sir. I've been taking notes ever since we got into the van," Bouldon replied obediently.

"I figured you were," Larcovic replied dryly. He was still feeling slightly disappointed with Bouldon's sarcastic comment during the team's briefing. The other members of the unit were well aware of Supervising Special Agent Gary Larcovic's occasional irritation with Bouldon. They remained silent. No one wanted to reawaken their boss's annoyance.

As they approached the crime scene, Larcovic saw two Sheriff's vehicles and several Arkansas State Police vehicles parked along-side the dirt road. Yellow "crime scene" tape surrounded a large portion of the woods. Pickering pulled the van up behind the Sheriff's car. A short, heavy-set man slowly climbed out of the vehicle to greet them.

"That's Sheriff White," said Pickering, beaming. "He's been Sheriff here for a long time. Y'all gonna find him very helpful and accommodating."

"Thanks for the ride and information, Deputy. You'd make a good tour guide if you ever want to change professions," he said, smiling.

Pickering chuckled, and then replied, "I'm assigned to you all day, sir."

When the agents got out of the van, Sheriff White walked over to the vehicle and introduced himself. "Good afternoon gentlemen, I'm Sheriff Cecil White. Welcome to Chicot County. As you will discover, we've taped off a wide section around the crime scene. Hopefully, we've preserved the area as pristine as possible to help with your investigation. The body was found late yesterday by a local hunter and his son. It's spring turkey season here in Arkansas. Normally, this area would be over-run by hunters for the next several weeks, especially on the weekends."

"Thanks for taping off the area, Sheriff. We appreciate how well you've preserved the evidence," Larcovic said shaking the Sheriff's hand warmly.

"We contacted the State Police. Their investigators and forensics people arrived from Little Rock several hours ago. The County just isn't equipped to handle this kind of case."

"I certainly understand. Am I safe in assuming your men and the troopers haven't unintentionally disturbed the evidence? I'm sure you know it's much easier to collect evidence, if there haven't been too many people moving around at the crime scene."

"Of course, of course," Sheriff White said nodding vigorously. "I hope things are not too messed up for y'all. We got a call from one of the Governor's staffers and they wanted us to be prepared for y'all's arrival. That's why we closed the road and used the tape."

"Thank you, Sheriff. I assume you've seen the corpse."

"Unfortunately, yes I did. It's the worst crime scene I've ever personally looked at. I've seen my share of murder victims over the years, but usually they die as a result of a stab wound or a bullet. Never seen anything like this before. I'm guessing the killer isn't local."

"What makes you think that, Sheriff?" inquired Bouldon, sounding a little surprised by the comment. He had been listening to the Sheriff's and Larcovic's conversation. "I'm agent Roger Bouldon," he said, extending his hand.

"Nice to meet you, Roger," said White.

"Roger is one of the Bureau's top criminal investigators," interjected Larcovic. He was mildly irritated with Bouldon's interruption, but didn't let it show in his voice. "He's been with the Bureau for a long time," he said, staring intently at his underling.

"I don't know for sure, Roger," Sheriff White replied mildly. "But this county is mostly a small, rural, farming community. I'd imagine there aren't too many people in Chicot that don't hunt. Everybody knows that spring turkey season started on April 8. These woods and this part of the county is where the majority of the birds are shot. Unless you are a total idiot, you wouldn't even consider being out in these woods to do anything but hunt, let alone kill somebody this way. You could get shot by a hunter! Locals know you wouldn't have any privacy, while half the county is out here turkey hunting. I can't even imagine the stupidest person in the county deciding to pick this spot. I think he would have gone outside the county somewhere to commit the crime."

"I see your point," said Bouldon. "That would make more sense."

"I'll be interested in what your team finds out," Sheriff White replied.

"Thanks for the driver and the information. We'll let you know as soon as we have anything," Larcovic assured the Sheriff.

"I'm thankful for your help." White began walking toward his squad car.

"Sheriff, is the body still in the woods?" Larcovic called at the Sheriff's receding back.

"No sir, the Coroner came out and picked it up before noon, today. I told him to take plenty of pictures of the corpse and the surrounding area. The victim was decomposing rapidly and the Coroner thought the body would be better preserved in one of his cold storage containers inside the morgue."

"Thanks again, Sheriff," Larcovic said looking a little downcast. "Damn!" He muttered to himself. *I wish they wouldn't have touched the body, until after we examined it. I'll bet the State Police investigators thought so too.*

Sheriff White turned back and asked, "Do you folks want to see the body first?"

"No, but our forensics expert, Dr. Peter Sloan, probably would. Can you have one of your deputies take him over to the morgue?"

"No need. I'll drop him off myself. I've got several

other duties to attend to today."

"Thanks again for your help and cooperation." Larcovic shook the Sheriff's hand warmly. "We'll see you back at your office later today."

"As busy as I am, I'll probably be there all night," White said, shaking his head with a tight grin.

"I've had those kinds of days too," Larcovic replied sympathetically. "I'll be in touch."

"Yes, sir." Sheriff White turned again and headed for his cruiser with Sloan trailing behind.

"Well men, let's get started with our investigation. Anthony, you and Roger can check for tire marks on the road. Even though it rained, the soil appears to be clay. Maybe we can get a clean tire mark, you never know. I'll take Frank and we'll examine the murder scene to see if we can find something there. Let me know immediately if you come up with anything significant."

As the team entered the woods, they saw a half-dozen State Police officers inspecting the area. Roger and Anthony broke off to study the road. It was apparent there was a significant amount of recent traffic on the road, despite being out in the middle of nowhere. All the tire marks on the road were run together and muddy. None of the tracks seemed to offer any usable evidence. Roger guessed the troopers had already come to the same conclusion. He stopped and scanned the area while Anthony continued down the road. He wondered, *where would I park a vehicle, if I didn't want to be seen? Not on the road; you'd be too visible there.*

A minute later Anthony yelled, "I think I see a small lane over here. I'm going to check it out."

"I'll be right there," Roger called back excitedly. When he caught up to him Anthony was already scanning the ground for tire marks. The ground was not very wet in this particular area of the woods. *The overhead tree limbs might have offered some cover from the rain*, thought Roger. He loved being an investigator looking for and finding evidence. It was like a game to him. Remembering that the Easter celebration had just concluded, he thought, *maybe that is why I always loved Easter as a child. I really enjoyed looking for the eggs.*

Several minutes later Anthony found a tire mark, which had been covered up by forest debris. "Go get Larcovic," he ordered Roger excitedly. *"He'll want to see this and make sure the lane is secure."*

Just then, one of the state troopers approached. "Hi, I'm Officer Sidney Johnson," he said as he edged around the debris to extend a hand to Rodriguez.

"Nice to meet you, Johnson. I'm agent Anthony Rodriguez, with the FBI."

"I was wondering what you found. Is it significant?"

"We got a fresh tire print. It might have been made by the unsub's vehicle. I'm about ready to make a tire tread impression mold. We brought a kit with us. But first, I'm going to wait for my partner, Roger Bouldon, and the rest of our team. My boss will want to see this before I proceed." he said authoritatively. "The rest of the team is over where the body was found."

"When you're finished with it, we'd like to have the mold," Johnson said in a serious tone.

"That's not up to me, but I'm sure we'll make it available to you," Rodriguez replied with a friendly smile.

When the team arrived at the lane, Larcovic asked Anthony, "Is it a good tire mark?"

"I've seen worse, but it's better than nothing. I'll take close-up photographs of it before I mold it." Rodriguez assured Larcovic. "How are you doing at the murder site?"

"We're doing fine. There's a lot of blood. It's spread all over the ground and on top of several small evergreen branches. We took samples and photographs, of course. Maybe some of it is from the unsub, but I doubt it. Probably it's from the victim."

"How about foot prints?" asked Rodriguez.

"We couldn't locate any. There is way too much forest debris, where the body was found," Giordano interjected. "It's full of pine cones, needles, dead leaves, and small branches. We also searched around the perimeter where the body was left. We didn't find anything there either."

"Neither did we," Officer Johnson put in. "We were hoping the body would still be in the woods to examine, but it was moved to the local morgue by the Coroner."

"Yes, that was very unfortunate. Who knows what we might have found, if it had been left untouched?" Larcovic asked rhetorically.

"By the way, I'm Arkansas State Police Detective Sidney Johnson. I've been put in charge of this investigation. I assume you're in command too," he said shaking Larcovic's already extended hand.

"Yes, I'm heading up the investigation for the Bureau. I'm Supervising Special Agent Gary Larcovic."

"It's a pleasure to meet you, Larcovic. I'm looking forward to working with the Bureau and I intend to offer reciprocal cooperation with your staff."

"I'm glad to hear that. Hopefully, between our two staffs we'll be able to resolve this case sooner rather than later. We're headed to the morgue to see the body."

"I've got several things to wrap up here and then we'll head over there too," Johnson replied.

"I hope our forensics expert has more to tell us. I'll see you at the morgue in a little while." As he turned away Larcovic thought, *I'm beginning to think Sloan's comment was quite accurate. There does not appear to be much evidence. I'm afraid this is going to be a very tough case to solve, but we will see.*

Bouldon came hustling up and said, "Boss, I've inspected several tree branches and I've noticed several of them have been recently damaged. Somebody was concerned about being seen or else they wouldn't have parked so far back in the lane. It was either our unsub, a hunter, or a kid using it to park with a girlfriend. But my intuition tells me it was the unsub."

* * *

Fifteen minutes later the team was heading back to the dirt road where the passenger van was parked and Deputy Pickering was patiently awaiting their return. "Deputy, would you please take us to the morgue? We're through here, at least for the time being."

"Yes sir, Agent Larcovic," Pickering replied dutifully. "I'm ready to leave whenever you are."

When they arrived at the morgue it was apparent Sloan had been busy examining the body, taking pictures, and writing notes for the investigatory case file. The covered corpse lay on top of a shiny, aluminum table in the middle of the room. Larcovic assumed it was their victim. "What have you learned?" he asked Sloan.

"Come over to the examination table. I think you will be pleasantly surprised. I'll show you why," Sloan said excitedly. "But first I'd like you to meet Dr. Gene Kelly. He's the County Coroner. He assisted me with the examination."

"Go ahead and remove the covering, Doctor, and show them her body," Sloan instructed. A second later, they saw a mangled corpse on the table. The agents were startled by what they saw. Her chest was punctured with more than a dozen stab wounds. It was obvious the unsub had used a highly corrosive chemical to try to destroy parts of her body. Her nipples had been peeled back exposing the tissue inside her breasts. In addition, her knee caps were smashed so badly her legs looked like they were almost separated. "Not to state the obvious, but it's clear she was severely tortured and then killed," Sloan said grimly.

"My god, what kind of monster does this?" Giordano

asked shaking his head with a look of surprised stupefaction.

"Someone that is a psychopathic killer," Bouldon answered coldly. "No doubt this isn't his first victim."

Sloan reeled off what he'd learned so far. "First of all, she died from being stabbed repeatedly in the heart and lungs. I'm sure she died very quickly, once the stabbing began. We're estimating that she'd been lying in that forest for a week or more. She was probably in her early twenties, maybe younger. As you can see, most of the facial tissues are gone, along with her fingers. Her teeth have been seriously damaged too. Our unsub used a very strong acid to hamper any identification. We may be able to get a partial plaster mold of her teeth, but I'm not sure how good it will be. I'm surprised the acid didn't totally destroy her teeth. I'm analyzing the acid sample. I would like to know what kind of acid he used. My best guess is hydrochloric acid."

"Excellent work, Peter," Larcovic said gratefully.

"We can take a DNA sample to try to identify her. This is a case where I hope our victim has been in trouble before," Sloan said with a shake of his head.

Bouldon sucked in his breath, looked at Sloan and nodded in agreement. "I concur."

"Yes, thank you. But surprisingly there is more." Sloan continued, "I also found what looks like a carpet fiber wedged in between her buttocks. She must have been squirming around on some kind of carpet to get fiber stuck in there. When we get back to Quantico, I'll turn it over to the lab for identification purposes. Presumably it's from the unsub's carpet. As for her nipples, the unsub either used a pair of pliers or vise-grips to try and tear them off her breasts. I think he used pliers, because they are not as cumbersome as vise-grips."

"Apparently, he had a knife. I wonder why he didn't use it to remove the nipples?" questioned Rodriguez.

"He probably intended to inflict the maximum amount of pain and not to remove them," suggested Bouldon.

"I think you could be right," Sloan replied. "However, I found something far more important. There was what I believe to be a small sample of dried semen just outside her vaginal canal on her labia minora. That, my colleagues, most likely gives us DNA evidence on the unsub." Sloan smiled broadly at his teammates.

"Wow! That's an amazing piece of luck!" Bouldon exclaimed. "Considering the extent to which he tried to conceal her identity – even using acid on her teeth – and then makes a boneheaded mistake like leaving semen on the victim. Does that make any sense?"

"Maybe he simply forgot and made an error," offered Rodriguez. "After all, he had a lot going on, from the looks of things. Maybe he just missed it and was unaware of the clue he left."

"Pack those samples away carefully, fellas. We'll take them with us, back to the lab," said Larcovic. "I hope our unsub has a record. If he does, we might be able to wrap up this case fairly quickly. Fingers crossed."

Chapter 7

The following Monday morning at 9:30 a.m., Michael Smith awoke rested and relieved that the long trip from Florida to Arkansas was concluded. He had overslept, but he didn't have any jobs scheduled as of yet; so, no problem. He cleaned up and put on a worn pair of blue jeans and a black NASCAR T-shirt.

Smith was hungry, but there wasn't enough food in the house to make a decent meal. He would have to eat out. There was not a single decent restaurant in Higden. He didn't relish the drive, but he decided it was a better option to drive over to Heber Springs, Arkansas, a half-hour away, for lunch and to pick up some groceries. In Heber Springs, there were more than a dozen restaurants and several grocery stores to choose from.

Sandy's Family Restaurant, located in downtown Heber Springs immediately came to mind. He had eaten there many times. Smith liked the owner and her delicious home-cooked meals. She liked him too and willingly traded meals for small jobs he could do for her.

He unlocked his light gray, 1999 Dodge Caravan, opened the door and slid into the driver's seat. The minivan started-up easily. He slowly backed out of the driveway and then abruptly stopped. He'd forgotten to attach his business signs to the vehicle. Smith got out and opened the minivan's back door, retrieved two magnetic business signs, and placed them on the vehicle's front doors. "Michael's Handy Man Services" was printed in big, bold, red letters along with his phone number. The signs were an inexpensive advertising tool to promote his construction businesses.

He could do most construction projects by himself, including those requiring electrical and plumbing expertise. But he would do whatever it took to please his clients, who knew him as, Michael Smith, when he was in Florida. Smith never used his former last name of Trettin in Florida, but in Higden, Arkansas he was still known as Michael Trettin. Generally, he just went by the name of Michael. He always insisted on being paid in cash. Occasionally, he would have to rent equipment or hire sub-contractors to help complete the jobs. Smith stayed busy, Monday through Friday, working on his customers' construction projects. On the weekends, he worked on his own stuff. The log cabin was finished inside and out, but he wanted to add an enclosed garage to the structure. That would be this season's project.

His annual routine was to leave Florida the first week of May. That way, he'd have plenty of time to arrive in Higden and attend the Homecoming and Decoration Day's events. He would leave Higden, the last week in October to go back to Florida for the winter. The schedule gave him ample time to complete his customers' jobs and his own. And, those annual trips back and forth from Florida to

Arkansas gave him enough time to hunt, capture, torture, and kill his victims. Many times, he killed more than one victim per trip.

On his drive to Heber Springs he admired the beautiful, northern Arkansas scenery, which included plush and dense forests, green-grassy pastures, and hilly terrain. There were small farm houses scattered along the roadway. An occasional larger home was visible on the curvy roadway too. Often, he would see a deer or two crossing the road or grazing in a nearby hilly field. It was a bright sunny day in Cleburne County on State Road 16. SR-16, aka Edgemont Road, was a relatively busy two-lane highway heading south out of Higden. During the weekends, the road was packed with visitors coming to fish or boat on Greer's Ferry Lake.

He wondered whether his latest victim had been found yet. He doubted it, but he would not have been shocked if she had. Smith liked to read any newspaper accounts of his killings. It made him feel important. Once the corpse was found in Chicot County, the Arkansas Democrat-Gazette in Little Rock would cover the story. People in Chicot County and most folks in Arkansas would be talking about the murder for days. Smith expected to read about his latest crime in The Sun-Times, the local newspaper serving Heber Springs. The newspaper was sold and distributed in the little hamlets, like Higden, in the Heber Springs area. He smiled with satisfaction remembering the story in The Sun-Times of the murder he committed last year in Ashley County.

When Smith read quotes from a newspaper's story

concerning one of his former murders, he would become irritated when the police spokesman got the facts wrong. If a reporter's account was spot on, he tingled with a perverse thrill reliving the kill. The local police in southern, rural counties were not nearly as experienced as the police in Little Rock. Most small-town cops and county sheriffs were not used to handling his type of killings. The newspaper articles in small local papers often exposed reporters' inexperience. But even when a newspaper account was poorly written, Smith always enjoyed reading about his kills. It not only made him feel important, it gave him a thrill thinking how he'd gotten away with another one.

As he drove toward Heber Springs, the realization that he had mistakenly left his latest victim in Arkansas rather than in Mississippi continued to bother him. Smith realized that he had been confused about the location of the state line. He tried to push the bothersome thought out of his consciousness. *What's done is done.*

Perversely, Smith became angry whenever a police spokesman was quoted in a newspaper describing one of the murders as "extremely gruesome" or in similar terms. It also pissed him off when the whores he killed were referred to as "innocent victims". *Hell, they weren't innocent! They were whores who deserved what they got, what I gave them.* Another pet peeve was when reporters referred to the perpetrator as a monster. *I'm not a monster,* he thought to himself, as he drove along Edgemont Road. *Take Jeffrey Dahmer; there's a monster for you. His victims were mostly innocents. Dahmer's homo-sexual victims were just seeking love and affection. Not only did Dahmer kill them, he dismembered their bodies, preserved some of their body parts, and eventually ate them. That's monstrous!*

Continuing in that line of thought, Smith told himself that his targets are lousy, low-life whores, who sell their bodies to the highest bidders and pass diseases to their John's. *I should be recognized for doing a valuable service for humanity by helping to get rid of them.* He gritted his teeth and mumbled to himself, *my victims are no better than my mother was. And she got what she deserved. Not by me. But I wish I had done it!*

It upset Smith when a reporter got the facts wrong, because he carefully planned his murders and followed a ritual in the elimination of the whores he chose. *Why weren't reporters as careful about their work as he was?* His obvious goal was to increase the intensity of their pain, torture them, and help them experience true punishment for their misdeeds. The only thing he was thankful to his mother for was setting an example for him by punishing him when she decided he had done something wrong. Her devotion to punishment for bad behavior had rubbed off on Smith.

But what she got wrong was that her cruel and violent beatings of him were not justifiable! Smith knew he had not led a perfect life as a minor, but most of the beatings he endured were undeserved. He theorized that the frequent beatings his mother inflicted on him were to atone for her own sins and miserable life. She blamed him and Emily Ann for all her troubles.

His Mother, Nancy Trettin, often complained that, if

she didn't have the two kids, she would be much better off. No doubt, it would have been easier for her to find a man to marry. Trettin was her given surname and she never married in spite of giving birth to the two children, Michael and Emily Ann. Nancy was fairly-attractive with bleached blond, curly hair and fascinatingly big, blue eyes. She was short with a well-proportioned figure. In high school she had the deserved reputation of being sexually promiscuous. Nancy was known as the class slut. Her father reacted to her promiscuity with an occasional thrashing or just ignoring her.

Of course, in the close-knit community of Higden the unwed birth of two children was a terrible embarrassment to Nancy's parents. They basically disowned her shortly after Michael was born, despite the fact that they were considered good church-going folk. Nancy had a string of low-end jobs, but turned to prostitution to provide for her and the two kids. Michael refused to accept that his mother was a prostitute in order to materially care for her children. And he certainly didn't think selling her body was noble or justifiable, even though it did put food on the table.

The good folks of Higden didn't buy Nancy's excuses either. They believed she really liked to party, get drunk, and be paid for sex. "Prostituting yourself sure beats working for a living," she'd tell her girlfriends. "Try it, you'll like it!"

Michael and his sister, Emily Ann, grew up not knowing who their fathers were. Nancy told them that they were only half-brother and sister. She claimed to know who their fathers were, but never disclosed the identities to her kids. Most of the towns-people thought Nancy's first boyfriend was responsible for Michael, but they had no idea who fathered Emily Ann.

When Smith could see the outskirts of Heber Springs in the distance, he noticed a newly built convalescent home on the right side of the road and a Holiday Inn under construction on the other side of the road. At the intersection of State Road16 and the main road leading into Heber Springs, there was a gas station, several retail stores, a bank, and a well-known local eatery.

Heber Springs, Arkansas, is a city with a semi-thriving economy and a population of around 7,000 people. It is the county seat of Cleburne County and its elevation is 341 feet above sea level. The city was named for its series of natural springs. Greer's Ferry Lake and the Little Red River are major tourist attractions for boaters, fisherman, and swimmers. Sugarloaf Mountain is on the eastern border of the city. The climate is characterized by hot, humid summers and generally mild to cool winters. Vacationers in Heber Springs have a choice of several motels, hotels, and bed and breakfasts. The area features, local restaurants, small tourist shops, resale shops, and an array of fishing, hunting, and boating specialty stores. There are very few chain stores in Heber Springs, with the exception of fast food places. Cleburne County is a dry county, dating back to the days of prohibition. If you want a drink in the county, moonshine is always available or liquor can be purchased in neighboring counties and brought in for consumption in private clubs or in the privacy of your own home. There are no stores in Heber Springs or Cleburne County where you can purchase alcohol.

Sandy's Family Restaurant was located in downtown Heber Springs. Smith pulled his weather-beaten Dodge minivan into a parking space in front of the restaurant and got out. *Over the past five years, I've used this vehicle to do some of my finest work.* He realized the Dodge Caravan was probably not going to last much longer. He planned to purchase another vehicle when he returned to Florida, depending on the season's profitability in Higden

When he entered the restaurant, he knew he'd made the right decision to make the half-hour drive. There was a delicious aroma of Sandy Darnell's home cooking permeating the restaurant.

The building was old, tattered, and worn. There were water spots on the ceiling. The tile floor was dirty and scuffed. It needed to be replaced. Some of the wallpaper hung loosely on the wall. Those signs of neglect of the building were what Sandy's customers saw when they came to her restaurant. However, the kitchen, counter-tops, tables, and chairs were all spotlessly clean. Still, Smith thought that Sandy really should remodel the restaurant. He knew she wouldn't, because the cost would be more than the business could afford. He chuckled as he thought to himself, *that's why I repaint the place every two or three years to freshen it up.*

Smith selected a seat at the counter, and the moment his butt made contact the familiar voice of Sandy Darnell came bellowing out from the kitchen. "Orders up!" she yelled. Seconds later, a stout, older woman came bustling out of the kitchen. She looked surprised when she saw him sitting there quietly. "When did you get back in town, Michael?" she asked with an affectionate smile.

"I arrived late last evening. I could hardly wait to see you," he said, returning her smile with a broad grin and acting as though it really mattered.

"I'm so glad you're back," Sandy said. "I've honestly missed seeing your narrow face, friendly smile, those beady dark brown eyes, and that awful looking goatee!" she replied mischievously. "Seriously, Michael, when are you going to shave?"

"Several months ago, I shaved it off. But I decided to grow it back after I realized I missed it. Don't you think it makes me look handsome?"

"Well, I guess if you like it, who am I to tell you otherwise?"

Smith smiled and nodded and then changed the subject. "Whatever you're cooking back there, it really smells delicious. I'm starving to death."

"It's today's lunch special, Swiss steak with gravy, mashed potatoes, green beans, and a roll, all for only five bucks. Want to try it?"

"Yes, I'll have the special, but please put extra gravy on the side," Smith said smiling at his plump hostess.

"Okay, one special with extra gravy on the side coming right up," she said returning his smile. She knew he'd like the food, no matter what she was serving. Most all of her customers were regulars. Sandy Darnell's reputation as the best cook in town was rightly deserved. The restaurant was always busy in spite of the condition of the building.

Sandy came to Heber Springs twenty years ago. She had little money, but knew how to cook food like no one else in town. Prior to opening her restaurant, she worked in Memphis, Tennessee for a master chef. Her boss felt sorry for Sandy due to her poor financial condition. He taught her how to cook as a way to help her out. Sandy worked long and hard for the master chef trying to repay his kindness with hard work and loyalty. When her mother passed away in the early 1980's, she returned to her hometown, Heber Springs, to handle the funeral arrangements. She never returned to Memphis. Starting and then running Sandy's Family Restaurant had been her life ever since.

When Sandy returned with Smith's order, he asked, "How's my favorite restaurateur?" Smith enjoyed their little inside joke that Sandy liked to call herself a restaurateur.

"Oh, I'm doing pretty well. I've got my challenges though," she replied with a frown.

"Unfortunately, we are all getting older, Sandy," Smith commented matter-of-factly.

Sandy's smile returned. She said, "Really Michael, I am glad you're back. I've got lots of things for you to do. I was thinking about calling a local contractor, but now I won't need too."

"Glad to hear it," Smith said. "I would have been pissed off, if you'd forgotten about me. After all, aren't I your favorite contractor or is that just a line of BS?"

Sandy laughed and said, "Don't you know you can't bullshit a bullshitter!"

"Okay, you're right," acknowledged Smith with a wry grin. "Give me a couple of days to get settled back in and I'll come over and take care of your projects. How's that sound?"

"Sounds good," she said as she poured him a hot cup of coffee.

"Thank you; you know I always need my morning cup."

"I totally agree. I don't know what I'd do without it," she said with a snort. "I got that habit from my Mama."

Quickly changing the subject, Smith said, "I see they're building a Holiday Inn out on 16. When did that get started?"

"Some outside firm, apparently from Little Rock came up here, got them a permit, and began construction several months ago. Most of the local trades are working there."

"You don't say. That ought to generate more business for me, if the trades are all tied up working on the hotel."

"I s'pose you're right. You're just plain lucky, aren't you?"

He nodded and said with an inward smile, "I sure am."

Several minutes passed before Sandy returned with the coffee pot to refill Smith's half-empty cup. "No charge today. I'll keep track and we can settle up when you finish my jobs." Before returning to the kitchen, Sandy said, "Don't worry, I really don't have that much for you to do, right now. I've been thinkin' about adding on. Could you handle that?"

"Sure, but I'd like to see the construction plans first."

"Well, I can show you my drawings," she responded.

"That will probably work," Smith said.

Several minutes later she returned with a slice of cherry pie ala mode on a warm plate. "It's gonna go to waste if you don't eat it," Sandy cracked.

Smith chuckled. "You know me too well, Sandy."

"Thanks honey. While you were chowing down on the special, I finished bakin' the pie, because I knew you'd like it with a scoop of ice cream." Her tone had become girlish and she gave her shoulders a flirtatious twitch which jiggled her ample breasts.

Smith knew she was just giving him some more BS. "Thank you," Smith said with a grin. "You know me too well." After he finished eating dessert, he waved a salute at Sandy and walked out to the minivan. *Next stop is the grocery and maybe the hardware store too,* he thought as he pulled out into traffic. He was pleased to be back in Arkansas. *People here are a lot more friendly and accommodating than in Florida. Maybe I ought to consider permanently moving back. It's been a long time since Nancy died. If Emily Ann is still alive, maybe I could find her and see how she's doing. Maybe we could get reacquainted again.* But then a twisted grin crossed his face as he thought about his true passion in life – killing whores. That might become more problematic and dangerous, if Emily Ann were around, he concluded.

Chapter 8

The day after the BSU unit returned from Chicot County, Larcovic summoned the team to the conference room for a briefing at 10:00 a.m. He was anxious to talk about the facts of the case and start developing a profile on the unsub.

When the team arrived, he said, "Please take a seat gentleman, we have a lot to review." He handed each team member a manila folder that included updated information concerning the progress of the on-going Chicot County murder investigation. "First, I will start with the bad news," he said frowning. "The DNA sperm sample found on the labia minora of the victim was not in our criminal database system. In other words, we don't know who he is. The blood samples found on and near the victim were her own. She was type-A negative, fairly rare."

"Is there any good news?" inquired Bouldon.

"Not exactly," said Larcovic. "We haven't been able to identify the victim either. But surprisingly, the Arkansas State Police laboratory did find two other miniscule sperm samples taken from inside her vaginal canal, stuck inside her uterus."

"Really!" Rodriquez exclaimed. "I assumed she was a hooker, judging from the looks of her bleached-blond hair, and heavy make-up. Not to mention the enticing fragrance of the cheap perfume still lingering on her dead body."

"Of course, it's been a problem to identify the girl due to her mutilated corpse. I'm not really shocked by that," Larcovic said glumly. "It's fair to assume she wasn't a local. Her blood samples indicated that she didn't have a police record and there were no missing person reports to pursue."

"What about the sperm samples?" Bouldon asked anxiously. "Were we able to identify any of those samples?"

"Yes, there was one found in the DNA database, but nothing on the other two," said Larcovic cautiously. "The problem is our match has an iron-clad alibi. Seems he was in Las Vegas with a girlfriend around the time of the crime. We're speculating he was the victim's pimp. Normally, a whore's pimp would be the natural suspect, when one of his whores is found murdered, but not in this case."

"Why not? What are the details on this guy?" Giordano piped up.

"Well Frank, he's black, a suspected pimp, and lives in a run-down apartment building right off I-82, which is one of the major red-light districts in Montgomery, Alabama. He does have an earlier charge for promoting prostitution, but it was dropped. The prosecutor's witness would not testify against him on the charge that he was promoting prostitution. There was an earlier burglary charge too, but nothing else. The guy's name is Daniel Jackson and he served four years for burglary in the Alabama Department of Corrections in Montgomery. After more than an hour of questioning, Mr. Jackson reluctantly told our investigator in Las Vegas that he had helped several young ladies with their careers," Larcovic said sarcastically. "But he denied knowing the victim and being a pimp for her or anyone else, for that matter. There is no way to prove he was her pimp, even though we think he probably was. Unfortunately for us, his story about being in Las Vegas during the relevant dates checks out."

"Were there any missing persons in Montgomery that resembled our victim?" Rodriguez asked.

"There were several persons reported missing, but none resembled our victim," answered Larcovic. "But I'll have someone check again."

"How did he explain the presence of his DNA inside her uterus?" Giordano asked. "Obviously, they would've had to have sexual relations sometime recently."

"According to Mr. Jackson, he has lots of parties and frequently has sex with women he doesn't know. Our investigator described the victim's appearance to him and showed him a picture of the corpse. Jackson claims he has no recollection of meeting her or sleeping with her either," Larcovic stated.

"What was the pimp's complete story, Gary?" Bouldon asked with a troubled look on his face. "The guy might be trying to cover his tracks by claiming he was in Vegas."

"Roger, I know you want to make sure nothing had been over-looked," Larcovic said appreciatively. "The Las Vegas police interviewed him, as well as our local agent there. The guy had copies of his airplane tickets to Las Vegas. It was several days before our experts believe the crime took place. And, a copy of his W-2G form, proving he'd won a large jackpot on slots at Binion's casino in downtown Las Vegas. After winning the jackpot, Mr. Jackson decided to stay for an additional week at Binion's on their nickel. Everything checked out. I wish it wasn't so, because we could wrap this one up fairly quickly. Unfortunately, our unsub is somebody else."

"Thanks for the clarifications, Boss," Bouldon said downcast.

"I'm fine with your questioning, Roger. I know you just want to help solve the case."

"What about the rest of the evidence, Boss? What have we learned?" asked Rodriguez.

"I am about to get to those items," Larcovic said. "First, we were able to get a match on the tire print. It is a 215/65R16 all-weather tire. They are typically used on Plymouth Voyagers, Dodge Caravans, and other similar makes and 1990's models. We were unable to locate the victim's missing finger nail and toe nail, at the crime scene. But maybe they were removed elsewhere. The indention marks on her nipples appear to have been made by a large type of pliers, possibly either electrical or the slip-joint variety. She had indentation marks on both her knee caps. It looks like the unsub might have used a small sledge hammer to break her knees."

"God that sounds painful, doesn't it? What about the stab wounds?" asked Rodriguez.

"Our forensics experts claim those wounds were made by either a large kitchen knife or a large hunting knife. The blade was calculated to be five to six inches long," Larcovic replied. "My gut tells me the wounds were made by a hunting knife."

"So, where does that leave us? Is our unsub a local or somebody from out-of-town?" asked Giordano. He was puzzled by Larcovic's assumption that the killing device must be a hunting knife. It surprised him that a senior agent would rely on his "gut".

"Of course, I can't be positive. But I think our unsub is not local. Sheriff White thought the unsub was definitely an out-of-towner. Remember his comment about it being turkey season when the murder took place."

"That made sense to me. I'd agree with his analysis," Bouldon interjected.

"Well gentlemen, that leads me to several other items that, before today, were unknown to us." Larcovic looked at Sloan and smiled. "Please tell them what our forensics team found out today about the victim."

"While we were analyzing some of the tissue samples, we discovered the victim had been given an above average dose of a powerful date-rape drug," Sloan said meaningfully. "The effects are fast acting and can be felt within minutes. The drug's chemical name is gamma hydroxybutyric acid. The government limited its use as soon as it was formulated by chemists working for the

Central Intelligence Agency. The drug's purpose is classified and the information about it is currently unavailable, even to us. However, I'm sure some form of it can be purchased - for a hefty price - on the black market. It's a very strong sedative. The liquid appears clear and it's odorless. The normal dose is one teaspoon for an average-size person. Our victim weighed less than 100 pounds. Two doses are excessive. If you're not careful with the dosage it can cause a patient to go into a coma," Sloan concluded.

"Thank you, Peter. Your description of the drug and its effects are helpful to our understanding of the unsub's technique." Larcovic went on, "I would not be surprised if that's how the unsub is able to control his victims. He probably offers them a drink laced with that drug and waits for them to become unconscious."

"Before I got here," Sloan said, "we just confirmed that the victim had a slight case of gonorrhea. No doubt the unsub by now has discovered he is having some pain when urinating. He'll need a strong anti-biotic to get rid of the symptoms."

Too bad for him, Bouldon thought angrily. *Somehow it doesn't seem like poetic justice when all the unsub gets is the clap, assuming he failed to use protection.*

"That's about all for now, gentlemen. I'd like you to start working on a profile of our killer. We need to drill down on this case. Let's help law enforcement catch this murderer!" Larcovic's voice carried the authority of an insistent plea from on high. He was pleased with the team's seriousness in their approach to the case. He knew they knew how important it was to solve the case as expeditiously as possible.

"Will do!" Rodriguez bellowed. "Boss, just let us know if there is anything else you want us to do, and we're on it!"

"Thank you, guys," Larcovic said as he looked around the circle of nodding heads. "I'll be giving you further updates as they become available. I'm very proud of your efforts. You're excused, gentlemen," he said as he closed his file folder. He stood and headed out the conference room door. Larcovic's mind had already turned to the need to update Director Underwood and contact that White House staffer. *They're both probably chomping at the bit for a progress report,* he thought as he walked to his office.

Larcovic was pleased with the direction the team was headed. They were making progress, but he knew they needed a break to blow the case wide open. *Let's just hope there's one out there,* he uttered in silent prayer as he picked up the phone.

Chapter 9

The team put its proverbial shoulder to the grindstone to fulfill Larcovic's instructions. It was their responsibility to develop a profile for the current serial killer based on the case evidence. Bouldon was assigned to take the lead and so he organized a team meeting in the conference room that afternoon. He invited Sloan, Rodriquez, Giordano, and Dr. Evangeline Landry, one of the staff psychologists, to attend the meeting.

Dr. Landry was a long-time friend and former lover of Bouldon's. He had encouraged her to join the BSU team years earlier. She became a valuable member of the staff. Landry wore stylish wire-rimmed glasses, which did not hide her deep brown eyes. She wore her hair long, and it flowed over her shoulders and down her shapely back. Dr. Landry was five-foot ten-inches tall, an impressive six-feet in heels. She was highly intelligent and an erudite scholar, yet personable and easy to work with. Landry was easy to look at and some of the guys enjoyed fantasizing about her.

Bouldon met her when they were both students at Tulane University in New Orleans. She was of French-Canadian decent, a direct descendant of 18th Century

Cajuns. Bouldon was over the moon for her when they first met. He truly fell in love with her after experiencing Evangeline's sexual prowess. But he also admired her wit and boundless energy. Aside from his desire to keep her close, Bouldon wanted her to participate in the profiling phase of the investigative process because of her expertise and talent.

When Giordano entered the conference room, he noticed Bouldon was already sitting at the table reading some papers. Giordano carried a pad of paper and a folder in one hand and a soda in the other. "Afternoon!" he said to Bouldon, who was staring at his notes for the meeting.

Bouldon looked up and managed to grunt a distracted "Hello". Bouldon had not yet really accepted Giordano as a member of the team. He would not have invited him to the meeting, except for Larcovic's insistence. Bouldon finally looked up and said, "You know, as James Cooper's replacement, you have some big shoes to fill. He was well-liked and was one of the finest special agents I've had the pleasure of knowing and working with. His loss was devastating to our team. I hope you will be able to do his job, but I doubt it."

Giordano was taken aback by the insult, but after collecting himself replied sincerely, "I'm very sorry agent Cooper was killed, but no one is irreplaceable. I'm sure he was a great FBI agent and deserved the respect you gave him. However, you don't really know me or my history in law enforcement. But let me assure you my commitment to the BSU and our group is rock solid. My whole body and soul have been nurtured and embraced by the law enforcement community. My uncle was a cop, my Dad was a cop, and I have a rich, broad background and experience in law enforcement. I've been an investigator in the FBI for over 20 years. If you review my body of work, I think you'll be satisfied with my competence to work on this case. I may have a different style and manner than you do. I rely on the facts, but I operate, work, and evaluate things based on a system I've developed. To some it may seem counterintuitive, because I don't just engage in fact-finding. I look for other things too. Sometimes, I look for the exact opposite of facts; meaning, I look for the things that aren't apparent in an investigation."

"Hmm, yeah, I know what you mean. I do the same thing. Some things are not readily noticeable on the surface," Bouldon agreed.

"I hate to say this, but your friend and co-worker died because there was someone on your team that didn't watch his back. Otherwise, he'd still be alive today. Mistakes are made and sometimes it's just fate that catches up to us. Anyway, I'd appreciate it if you don't try to intimidate me. And I expect you not to convey your negative opinions about my worthiness to the rest of the team."

"Fair enough, but you're going to have to prove your worth to the team to win my respect. So far, you're doing alright, but I want to see more," Bouldon said undeterred from his judgmental attitude toward the newest member of the team.

"I'll do my best and that should be more than enough," Giordano replied carefully hoping to end the confrontation. "Be patient and give me an opportunity to prove my worthiness." Giordano knew he didn't really have to prove himself to Bouldon or any of the others on the team. Underwood and Larcovic had confidence in him or he wouldn't have gotten the job. Still, he couldn't help resent Bouldon's cocky attitude and he steeled himself to prove he deserved his place on the team.

When Sloan and Rodriquez arrived, they could sense tension in the room. Bouldon's face was red and Giordano's usual friendly composure had vanished. They both assumed Bouldon must have tried to intimidate the new guy, as was his custom. They hoped Giordano had not backed down and had defended himself adequately. Otherwise, there would be further tension on the team which was not helpful. They dreaded the thought of Larcovic having to get involved to settle matters. They had paid for Bouldon's indiscretions before and didn't want to see that show again.

Trying to look like he was unaware of the tension between his colleagues, Rodriquez nodded to Bouldon and said with a sly grin, "I see you two got here early. Have you figured everything out by now? Do we really need to have this meeting?"

Bouldon shook his head and responded without returning the smile, "No, but we have some similar thoughts on the case. Better come in. We are going to need all the help we can get."

A minute later Dr. Landry entered the conference room. The men on the team who knew her were all looking forward to her arrival to see her attractive figure in the stylish dresses she wore. Dr. Landry did not disappoint them. She greeted all the participants, lowered herself onto a chair, and adjusted her wire-rim glasses. "Gentlemen, I'm sorry to be late, but I had to take an important telephone call."

"No problem, Evangeline," pronounced Bouldon. He still longed to be with her, but she had made it abundantly clear when she joined the BSU staff that their former romantic relationship would not be rekindled. Their relationship would be strictly business. Bouldon briefly spoke about the importance of this phase of the operation and encouraged all the participants to join in the discussion.

Dr. Landry spoke first, saying, "Obviously, this was not a crime of passion. The unsub stabbed his victim a dozen times after he had methodically tortured her. He sexually abused her before the torture began. He raped her and then tortured her by trying to extract or crush her nipples. I cannot fully understand or explain his motives, but I believe his actions had more to do with dominance rather than sex. Serial killers motivated by the will to dominate tend to be very methodical and organized. Typically, they were victims of abuse during childhood, which causes them to feel inadequate and powerless as adults. These serial killers have a tendency to murder not for lust, but for power and control. It suggests that he might have chosen this victim, because she reminded him of someone he knew, despised, or hated – perhaps a girlfriend, sister, aunt, or even his mother. Until we know his history some aspects of his motive will remain a mystery."

"His M.O. is indicative of a well-thought out plan,

probably done by an experienced killer," commented Bouldon. "Judging from the available evidence, I'd suggest we're looking for someone who is either in his late thirties or mid-forties. He's a white male, who was outside his home territory. He might be an over-the-road trucker or someone who carries tools for his occupation, maybe a construction worker. Most people don't carry a sledge hammer in their tool boxes."

"I'd guess he was abused or traumatized in his childhood by a parent or guardian. Our unsub most likely came from a broken home and was raised by a single parent. Probably criminal behavior was displayed on a regular basis," added Landry. "Also, I believe our unsub is of above-average intelligence based on the fact that he has not been caught. I think we will find he has killed many victims over a period of years. This guy is not a rookie. He's a successful serial killer."

Giordano cleared his throat and interjected, "I believe our unsub is fairly strong, due to the fact that there were no drag marks on the ground at the crime scene. He must have carried the victim from his vehicle to the kill site. It's quite a distance from the vehicle through the pine forest to the clearing."

Rodriquez stated, "Based on the tire print found in the lane, I'd suggest he drives a 1990's late model Plymouth or Dodge minivan. The minivan is probably not painted a bold color, because he doesn't want to attract any undue attention. For instance, he wouldn't have a bright shiny red vehicle that would be easily remembered. The unsub would probably choose a vehicle painted in a dark color, like black, brown, or gray."

"Since we seem to agree he is fairly smart, I would guess he picked the location due to its rural nature, off a main road and in the middle of nowhere, for a particular reason," Giordano suggested. "I'd say, judging from the condition of the body, our unsub requires a considerable amount of time to do his work. I agree that he is not from southern Arkansas or Chicot County, based on Sheriff White's comments concerning the opening of the Spring Turkey season. Further, I doubt if he were ever in the military. His actions are more indicative of someone who has a severe personality disorder. We haven't been at war for thirty years, so I doubt he could have passed the psych test required for recruitment into the military. If he got past the recruiters, given a severe personality disorder, he wouldn't have made it through basic training."

"This young girl was most likely a prostitute," Bouldon pointed out. "I'd guess our unsub is not married and probably doesn't have a girlfriend. I wonder if he seeks out hookers for sex or if there is something more to it than that. Any ideas on that subject?"

Sloan responded, "It appears that our unsub is very methodical, but there is something about his methodology that is puzzling. Why does he remove only one finger nail and not others? Likewise, why only one toenail? Why does he injure both of her nipples and both of her knee caps? His actions seem to be systematic, so there are probably other victims with similar injuries. There is a peculiar pattern to his approach which must have some significance to the unsub, but I can't figure it out yet," Sloan concluded with a puzzled look on his face.

Giordano injected another thought. "Why did our unsub go to great lengths to try to disfigure the body? Undoubtedly, he knows that he can't destroy all her DNA information, unless he burns up the body. Why use the acid on her face, teeth, and hands? But then leaves his own DNA in the form of sperm outside her vagina. Lady and gentlemen, there must be a reason for that, but I can't figure out what it might be."

"Maybe it's kind of a message he is leaving to the authorities, unconsciously telling them who was responsible for the prostitute's death," Dr. Landry speculated. "He may or may not be aware, but it appears to be an unwritten pronouncement of him taking responsibility for the crime."

"It's interesting that our victim appears to have been from the Montgomery, Alabama area," Rodriquez chimed in. "Yet, there is no record or information that can confirm she was from there. That young woman could have been from anywhere inside or outside the United States. But without being able to ID her, it's as if she never existed."

"Our most recent update received from the Arkansas State Police laboratory indicated they thought she had a recent abortion," reported Sloan. "Our laboratory performed a toxicology exam on her tissues and, not surprisingly, discovered she was taking a contraceptive drug to avoid pregnancy."

There was a moment of silence. Bouldon looked around the table to see if anyone had anything to add.

Since no one spoke up, he decided it was time to wrap up the meeting. "Well, I've been taking accurate notes of our observations and thoughts. I'll give the notes to Ms. Coughlin and ask her to type them up and distribute them to you later today. Once you receive the notes, take the rest of the day to study them. We'll get back together in the morning to prepare a profile on our unsub. Thank you for your patience and input."

Chapter 10

Early the following morning, Larcovic and Bouldon sat at the conference room table discussing the team's meeting, which Bouldon had led. They were analyzing the data and trying to develop a profile of the unsub. Larcovic's secretary, Sarah Coughlin, knocked on the door, cracked it open, and said, "You've got an urgent call from Sheriff Cecil White of Chicot County, Arkansas on line one. I think you should take it," she said.

"Thank you, Sarah, I'll take it here." Larcovic pushed the number one button on the telephone console. "Sheriff, this is supervising special agent Larcovic. What have you got?"

"I think we've got a tape of him and the vehicle he was driving!" Sheriff White shouted into the phone.

"Sheriff, are you talking about the killer?" Larcovic asked excitedly.

"The killer!" Sheriff White sounded like he was about ready to bust.

"Calm down, Sheriff," cautioned Larcovic. "I don't want you to have a heart attack or stroke."

"The night of the murder, we got him on a video tape at a gas station not far from where the body was found."

"Where is the station located and can you get me a copy of the video tape showing our suspect?" Larcovic asked enthusiastically.

"It looks as if he stopped north of Lake Village, Arkansas at a truck stop to fill up his gas tank. Lake Village is less than ten miles from the pine woods, where the victim was found. I already gave the tape to the Arkansas State Police. I'm sure they will make a copy for you. The gas station is equipped with a multiple video taping system. Unfortunately, it is not in good repair. However, the officer who reviewed the video tape said our suspect, who was pumping gas, appeared to be hiding his face from the camera. He was wearing a ball cap and sun glasses."

"Were you able to make out the license plate number and the make and model of the vehicle?" Larcovic asked anxiously as he crossed his fingers hoping for a positive reply.

Pausing briefly to collect himself, Sheriff White said, "Yes, the vehicle was a 1999 Dodge Caravan. The tape is in black and white format, so the officer who viewed the tape could only say the vehicle was a dark color and the paint appeared weathered or dirty; hard to tell which in black and white. He reports that there were many specks of dirt covering the vehicle's side and tires. We're guessing the dirt was clay, judging from the area."

Larcovic was so excited he pumped his fist up and

down and nearly shouted "Yes!" in triumph.

Sheriff White continued, "The license plate was a custom-made plate with 'Alabama' shown on the top and 'Crimson Tide' on the bottom. It's a University of Alabama customized commemorative plate. Those plates have red lettering on the top and bottom with black numbers and letters, on a white background. The license plate number is JDW 2498 and it expires on June 2004. The vehicle is registered to James 'Dutch' Williams of Eufaula, Alabama. He is 46-years old, a Marine Corps veteran of the 1st Gulf War, also known as Operation Desert Storm. We contacted the authorities in Eufaula. We learned that the plate was reported stolen a week before we found the victim in the pine woods."

"This information sure sounds like the break we have been hoping for," Larcovic said enthusiastically.

"There's more. A homeless man was searching for food in the trash bin behind the same truck stop, when he made a startling discovery. He noticed a black plastic trash bag that had blood leaking out of it. Thinking it was raw meat, he opened the bag. But what he found inside was a blood-soaked tarp, a regular-size towel, a hand towel, and an empty bottle of water, all coated with dried blood. I wouldn't be surprised if it's our victim's blood."

"That will be easy for the Arkansas laboratory to determine," commented Larcovic.

"The driver of the Dodge went inside the station to pay his fuel bill, which, incidentally, he paid for in cash. Unfortunately, the video recording machine inside the building was broken and needed to be repaired or replaced. Sadly, we were not able to get a close-up of his face."

"Well, at least we have the outside video tape intact. Can you send a copy of the tape to our BSU laboratory in Quantico, Virginia? "I'm sure our technicians will be able to improve the tape's quality."

"Sorry, I can't make a copy for you, but the Arkansas State Police have that capability. I'm sure they will gladly send you a copy."

"Thank you, Sheriff. We will be anxiously awaiting the arrival of the tape. Is there anything else?"

"Not really, but you might be interested to know that the gas station was sold prior to the murder and the new owner ordered a new video system. Regrettably, the new system is scheduled to be installed next week. That's all I have to report for now. I really appreciated working with you, Agent Larcovic."

"Thank you again for all your help, Cecil. It's been a pleasure working with you as well, and becoming acquainted with your staff. But hopefully, our paths won't cross again in the near future."

"Come back and visit us on your next vacation. It'd be nice to cast some flies with you, Agent Larcovic, but I don't want to see any more cases like this one."

"I don't either, but we'll be in touch," Larcovic said slowly hanging up the phone while looking thoughtfully into the distance. He knew the case wasn't solved yet, but this was real progress. He picked up the telephone and called Underwood to update him on the status of the case.

After Underwood heard Larcovic's report, he asked, "May I assume you are going to be talking with Mr. Williams in Eufaula, Alabama fairly soon?"

"No, not personally, I've got some research to do first. I'll probably call our office in Montgomery and ask them to pay a visit to Mr. Williams and have them do a preliminary assessment of him. It's possible he might be trying to cover up his involvement in the case by reporting the plate as stolen." After Larcovic finished his report to the Director he promised, "I'll keep you posted with our ongoing progress."

"I'm very pleased with you and the team, Gary." Underwood replied warmly. "Keep me in the loop."

"I will," Larcovic assured the Director before hanging up the telephone. Larcovic thought about approaching Williams too, but decided to wait until he learned what the Alabama field office had determined. In the meantime, Larcovic called his contact at the Department of Defense to obtain Sergeant Williams's service record.

The record revealed no disciplinary issues. Sergeant Williams received a medical discharge after being seriously injured during Operation Desert Storm in January 1991. The record also indicated that Sergeant Williams was African-American. He was retired and receiving disability benefits. Larcovic also noted that Williams required a wheelchair ever since returning home from the Walter Reed National Military Medical Center in Bethesda, Maryland.

* * *

Five hours later, the long-awaited field report arrived from the Montgomery FBI office. Interestingly, Williams owned a dark maroon-colored, 2000 Dodge Caravan. However, on the date of the murder the vehicle was in a repair shop to fix a crushed fender. The interviewing agent stated that the plate was probably stolen when it was in the body shop. And, the report concluded that it would be highly unlikely Mr. Williams had any involvement in the crime.

Larcovic was disappointed with the report, insofar as he'd hoped for an easy catch by connecting Williams to the crime. On the other hand, he was sort of relieved that a Purple-Heart vet was not involved. He called Underwood to report what he'd learned.

At precisely 3:30 p.m., Rodriquez, Giordano, and Landry were summoned to the conference room by Larcovic. The agents assumed they were being summoned to formulate a profile on their current unsub. When the three agents arrived, Larcovic and Bouldon were already looking over a document together and drinking coffee. Larcovic quickly stood up from the table, looked at the agents, and said, "Good afternoon." He invited them to take a seat and in a serious tone added, "After reviewing the case materials, and your analysis and comments, I think Roger and I have settled on a profile for the unsub that our joint efforts have produced. I've talked with Director Underwood about the profile and he is in complete agreement with my decision to issue a nation-wide alert.

Over the last several days, between our investigative efforts, the Arkansas State Police, and the Chicot County Sheriff's Department, we believe we have enough credible evidence to inform law enforcement agencies nationally about this matter. And, we are ready to ask for their assistance."

Larcovic continued, "Before we release the profile of our unsub, I'd like to go over the reasoning behind some of the information we will present. As you know, the majority of serial killers are male. The video tape from the truck stop bears that fact out, assuming the driver is our unsub. The tape clearly shows him to be a white male. Since our other two potential suspects were black, they are being ruled out. Further, we believe the evidence found in the station's trash bin proves that the unsub was there at the relevant time. In addition, the video tape showing the white man wearing a ball cap and dark sunglasses pumping gas reveals his intention to try to avoid the video camera. Wearing sunglasses two hours prior to day break is suspicious behavior. So, based on his choice of clothing - the T-shirt and ball-cap - both depicting a NASCAR theme, we have concluded the unsub is probably a younger man. Couple that fact with speculation that our supposed perpetrator has been doing these killings over a long period of time probably means he's in his late thirties to early forties."

Larcovic looked around the room at the assembled group of agents and went on, "The video tape evidence and our technicians' calculations indicate our unsub's height to be approximately five-foot nine-inches tall. He appears to be of medium build and the estimate of his weight is 175 pounds. The man on the tape pumping gasoline has dark hair and sports a neatly trimmed goatee."

Bouldon raised his hand and interjected, "May I make a comment?"

Larcovic gave Bouldon a sharp look, but replied mildly, "Sure, everyone is welcome to contribute, but please wait to speak until after I've finished reviewing with you all the material."

Bouldon shrugged his shoulders, took a deep breath, and settled back in his chair. Bouldon's air of self-confidence remained intact, but the others knew Bouldon's ego was a bit deflated by Larcovic's gentle put down.

Larcovic resumed his exposition of the accumulated evidence. "In the video tape our suspect was wearing a 2000 Daytona-500 T-shirt. We're speculating here, but I think our unsub might reside in Florida. Incidentally, the number-3 ball-cap he was wearing commemorates the legendary NASCAR driver Dale Earnhardt. Earnhardt died in a terrible crash at the Daytona International Speedway in Florida February 2001. The video from the gas station shows our suspect drives a dark-colored 1999 Dodge Caravan with weathered paint. Since a sledge hammer was apparently used as part of the torture kit, we believe the suspect works in some type of construction. You don't carry a sledge hammer in your tool box unless it's used frequently."

"So," Larcovic lowered his voice and glanced around the room again, "Within the next few hours we will be releasing the alert concerning our suspect. The document will state, 'FBI Alert: We are looking for a suspected murderer, who is a white male, with brown or black hair, sporting a neatly trimmed goatee, about five-feet nine-inches tall, weighing approximately 175 pounds. Probably works in the construction industry and drives a dark-colored, weathered 1999 Dodge Caravan. The vehicle may have a Florida license plate. The suspect was last seen wearing NASCAR commemorative clothing and was recently spotted a week ago in southern Arkansas. Consider this individual to be armed and extremely dangerous. Approach with caution and do not try to apprehend him by yourself. Report any sightings to the FBI's BSU office in Quantico, Virginia.'

"Before I open the meeting up for discussion, both the Director and I want to thank you for your hard work on this investigation. Both of us feel sincerely fortunate to have such fine people working for us. As part of the process, I'd like you to consider several questions concerning this alert. First question, does anyone in this room think our assumptions are incorrect? Second question, do you think this alert would disclose too much information? Let me point out that the only two things we know specific to our unsub is that he drives a 1999 Dodge Caravan and he sports a dark-colored goatee. The rest of the data could apply to millions of people, since we don't have a clear picture of his face. And finally, I think it's the right decision to involve the law enforcement authorities at this time, but do you? I won't be offended if you disagree. I want comments from each of you, starting with Roger."

"Well, before I say anything about the alert, I'd also like to thank the members of our team for their help,"

Bouldon said nodding appreciatively. "As to my opinion, I think our profile is accurate, but we should wait a little while longer before we release this information. It would be better if we could confirm several of the assumptions. For some reason, the press always seems to obtain confidential case information early from the authorities and prematurely releases the information to the general public. If the profile is released too hastily, it might make our unsub uneasy and affect his actions in the future."

"Good point, Roger." Larcovic said matter-of-factly.

The next to speak was Rodriquez. "I guess I partially agree with your decision. However, I really think it would be better, if we could absolutely verify the guy pumping gas was the same person who dumped the trash bag into the bin. Surely, there has got to be either another witness or video tape we could use to back-up the assumption."

"Maybe I should give Sheriff White a call and have him look around some more. It's possible something significant could have been over-looked," Larcovic responded thoughtfully.

"The Arkansas police have already been able to verify that the victim's blood was found inside the trash bag," Sloan put in. "I've been racking my brain concerning the unsub's M.O. and I've come up with a theory. I think he is trying to torture his victims in such a manner as to gradually increase their pain. Breaking someone's knee cap would be enough pain in and of itself to render a victim unconscious. I believe his goal, sick as it may be, is to allow his victims to suffer the greatest amount of pain up until the time he kills them. I say we wait for more evidence to present itself before we issue the alert."

"That seems logical to me," Landry said with a nod. "I assume we all agree this victim was not his first. I'd assume also he has experimented with his M.O. over the years and has tweaked it accordingly. But if Director Underwood and you believe we need to elicit more help, then go ahead and do it."

"I'd hoped for slightly more support for my plan," Larcovic said half-heartedly. "Giordano, what do you think? Should we wait, as some of the others suggest?"

Giordano cleared his throat and then spoke in a cautious tone. "Well, in my experience I've found it's not always wise to rely on too many assumptions. For example, I think you indicatcd the two things you thought were revealing about our unsub depend on whether or not the driver of the Caravan is the unsub. Don't misunderstand me, I believe he is our unsub. But I want to be absolutely sure. Dodge made millions of the 1990 era Caravans. They were offered in various shades of black, gray, red, blue, green, and white. Gray is a popular color, but describing the vehicle is gray is based on an assumption. Maybe it is actually black. But, let's suppose our unsub was driving either a gray or a black vehicle. We can't pick up every male driving a 1999 Dodge Caravan in the southern part of the country. There were at least a million of them manufactured. The fact that the driver has a dark goatee is significant, but only if he is the unsub. How many men wear beards, particularly in the south? I think we are a little premature in releasing this information, but I really don't think it would hurt. As far as

I can see, nobody here has a better idea. Meanwhile, we can continue with our investigation."

"Frank, for a rookie I think your logic makes pretty good sense. I agree with you. We might be looking for the wrong man," said Larcovic. He paused briefly and then spoke again. "Okay, let's do it. I'm willing to take a chance and see where it gets us," he said and smacked the table with the palm of his hand. Larcovic looked into the eyes of the men and woman seated at the table, and then concluded with an air of resignation. "I don't know if there is a better option or not, but I'm hoping Lady Luck might be on our side for a change."

Chapter 11

Several weeks later on a Monday morning, in Higden, Arkansas, Smith picked up a copy of The Sun-Times, the Heber Springs newspaper. To his astonishment there was a story and a profile of the suspected killer, who had left the body of a young woman in a Chicot County forest weeks before. He was especially interested in the FBI profile released by the Arkansas State Police identifying the suspect as a white male, late thirties to early forties, 5-foot 9-inches tall, and 175 pounds. The article claimed the suspect drives a dark-colored 1999 Dodge Caravan, possibly with a Florida plate. He was last seen wearing NASCAR clothing and has dark hair with a goatee. The suspect may work in the construction industry. The story referred to the suspect as someone who should be considered armed and dangerous. It further stated that the public should avoid contact and report any sightings of the suspect to the FBI's BSU office in Quantico, Virginia. The profile was extremely accurate, he thought nervously. He wondered if they had a picture of his face too. *What the hell am I going to do? Where will I hide? How soon will it be, before I'm identified and arrested?*

Smith almost panicked when he looked over at his vehicle and saw the Michael's Handy Man Service sign, which included his phone number, on both front doors of his Dodge Caravan. He quickly removed the signs and put them into the back of the vehicle. It's time to purchase another minivan, he thought. Half an hour later, he was home looking through the northern Arkansas auto trader's magazine. After locating a 2002 Toyota Sienna in Clinton, Arkansas, he contacted a close neighbor and asked for help getting him to the dealership. Smith explained that his engine had blown up and his vehicle was no longer drivable. He parked the Dodge in a back corner of his property, removed the Florida plate, the business signs, and tools from the back of the Caravan. After covering the Dodge with a large canvas tarp, he placed the signs, tools, and the plate in a storage room inside his house. Still distraught, he shaved off his goatee and hid his NASCAR clothing under linens at the back of a dresser drawer in his bedroom.

As predicted by FBI agent Roger Bouldon, the FBI Alert was released prematurely. The local newspaper did, indeed, provide Smith the warning he needed to avoid being identified by local authorities and arrested. Smith thought no one in Higden would ever suspect him of being a murderer, because he was local and liked.

* * *

That afternoon Smith called the Toyota dealership and

made an appointment to visit their used car lot the following morning. He'd researched what a fair price for a 2002 Sienna was prior to going to the dealership. The salesman he talked with assured Smith he would get the best price the dealership could offer.

* * *

The following morning Smith spent over an hour haggling for a better deal with the salesman, who seemed accommodating yet kind of cagey. The guy was typical of most auto salesman, Smith thought. But he decided to buy a 2002 Sienna that had not been previously advertised for sale. The Sienna he bought had just been traded-in by an elderly couple. After he gave it a test drive, Smith was satisfied the vehicle was in excellent mechanical condition. The body had several small blemishes, but the tires and battery were like new. Over all, the car was perfect for his needs. The color was an unusual shade of dark blue, and it had low mileage. The salesman was willing to sell the vehicle for less than market value due to the color and the fact that Smith said he didn't need a warranty. Smith agreed to buy it as is without any reconditioning. He was happy to have found it so quickly. Smith paid $5,000 down and financed the rest through Toyota Credit Corporation. During the test drive, Smith noticed that the Sienna had a softer ride than the Caravan. The salesman said that was one of the advantages of a Toyota.

Shortly after arriving home, Smith removed the rear

seats and put them in the storage room inside the house. He thought about replacing the signs, but decided against it. The dealership had given him a paper license plate to use for up to forty-five days. He called the License Bureau in Florida and reported that his plate had been stolen. The clerk in Florida told him they'd issue a new number and plate, but Smith needed to first send them a check for the replacement.

* * *

Later in the afternoon Smith sat in his easy chair contemplating his FBI profile. Smith felt somewhat relieved by his quick actions. He had a newer vehicle, made by Toyota not Dodge, and the vehicle was a different color. The goatee was gone. By now, he was sure the authorities had discovered that there was a stolen Alabama license plate on his former vehicle, when he arrived in Lake Village, Arkansas, the night of the murder. Undoubtedly, the owner of the Alabama plate had been contacted and interviewed. What a shock that must have been for the owner, he thought, chuckling to himself. He replaced his NASCAR T-shirts and ball-cap with Heber Springs fishing T-shirts and a cap. He also planned to wear his University of Arkansas football gear. After reviewing the situation, Smith thought there was nothing more that could be done. In the future, he decided to leave the crime scene more quickly and distance himself at least two or three hours before stopping for the night. It would probably make more sense to refuel before picking up a victim to avoid the need to stop afterward for fuel.

* * *

On Wednesday afternoon, Smith began his work at Sandy Darnell's restaurant. As promised, Sandy had some minor repairs for him to do. He worked through most of them by Friday afternoon. Fortunately for Smith, he had scheduled several other jobs in Higden which he could start working on the following week. He decided to delay starting the addition to his garage due to lack of finances. Risk management was more important than his desire to have a garage, at least for the time being, he thought. He planned to finish his work at Sandy's by Saturday afternoon. If he could get enough jobs in Higden during the season, the additional money might allow him to do the foundation and possibly frame the garage before leaving Higden in the fall. Smith had some additional funds in Florida, but not in the bank. He didn't have any way to access them until he returned to St. James City.

When Sandy saw the new vehicle parked outside her restaurant, she asked Smith, "I thought you drove a gray minivan?"

Anticipating any obvious questioning concerning the new vehicle, he said, "I did up until the time the engine quit working. It was about time to buy a different vehicle anyway."

"What did you do with the old one," Sandy inquired.

"It's parked at my house for the time being. Thought I'd keep it and maybe someday put a different engine in it. I tried trading it in, but the dealership wasn't going to give me much for a vehicle that doesn't drive," Smith responded matter-of-factly.

"Well, I see you finally took my advice and shaved that growth off your face. The beard didn't make you look very good," Sandy said with a triumphant look.

"I got tired of trimming it and it sometimes itched. I might grow it back, but not right now," Smith said with a shrug of his shoulders. "Several of my lady friends in Florida complained about the beard when I kissed them."

"Who might they be?" asked Sandy with mock curiosity.

"Just several girl friends of mine - you don't know them."

"I thought you said you'd kind of given up on women for the time being?" Sandy asked inquisitively.

"Generally I have, but occasionally a man has needs, you know," Smith replied with a touch of irritation in his voice.

"I'd agree with that. Unfortunately, I never found a man that I wanted to be with who could also satisfy *my* needs," Sandy said with a sly smile on her face.

Quickly changing the subject, Smith said, "Since I depleted my funds, I will be working on weekends to try and catch up. I should be finished with your job later today."

"That sounds good to me. If you come in for breakfast on Monday, we can settle up."

"I'll be here Monday morning, first thing. I've got another job lined up for Monday afternoon. Will that work for you?"

"Yup, you come in again Monday morning, Michael, and yer breakfast will be hot and ready," she said and gave him a brazen wink.

Smith was relieved to get away from Sandy and get to work. He set up his wallpaper table inside the restaurant and began replacing the worn wallpaper that was practically falling off the walls. But just a few minutes later, Sandy reappeared and began to inspect his work. Her excessive curiosity about his business and looks slightly rattled Smith. He wondered whether she suspected anything. Maybe she had read the story in the newspaper about the slaying in Chicot County and the FBI profile. He tried to shake off his feeling of discomfort. She was probably just trying to be flirtatious, he told himself.

Trying to appear casually confident by making conversation, he asked, "Do you like the way the wallpaper looks?"

"Well, I think so, but I'm not sure. I hope my customers like it," she said.

"Don't kid yourself, Sandy; they aren't coming in here to eat because of the wallpaper. Your delicious recipes are what keep them coming back for more," Smith replied enthusiastically. "Relax. The wallpaper will look much better than it does now and you'll like it."

Almost immediately, Smith noticed a change in her attitude. Apparently, she was actually very anxious about how the wallpaper was going to look. He decided that was the problem and it had nothing to do with the murder in Chicot County. Her flirtatiousness was probably just her way of dealing with a little anxiety. Smith was relieved. He didn't want to eliminate Darnell. He would, if necessary. But he didn't relish the idea.

* * *

Later that night, he thought about Darnell again. He concluded their friendship would not allow her to suspect him, unless the evidence was absolutely indisputable. She would not come to the conclusion on her own that he might be a murderer. Smith thought Sandy felt close to him and he had already bullshitted her enough to make her think he really cared about her. In the future, he intended to monitor her degree of questioning about the vehicle and the beard. If she dropped those subjects, he could assume it was safe not to consider Sandy a threat. If not, he'd quickly plan her demise. Killing her would be the easy part. The challenge would be to make it appear to be an accident.

Chapter 12

Smith could hardly wait to attend Homecoming Day and Decoration Day weekend, which began Saturday, May 15, 2004 in Higden, Arkansas. Recently, he'd talked to two cousins who said they were coming to join him at the festivities. He wondered if Emily Ann might show up for the celebrations. Smith was not very optimistic about seeing her. His cousins told him it had been years since they'd last seen her in Higden. Smith planned to attend the all-day picnic at the park. Attendees were expected to bring a dish to share. Smith wasn't much of a cook so he asked Sandy Darnell to make a bowl of southern potato salad, so he would have a dish to contribute to the picnic. Sandy gladly whipped up the dish for him. She refused to accept his money for making the salad. He purchased a small American flag from the Veterans of Foreign War's lodge and planned to place it at his grandfather's grave stone on Sunday.

Smith arrived early at the park. He looked forward to seeing his two cousins. It had been quite a while since he'd seen them in person. Usually, he only called them on Thanksgiving or Christmas to say hello and wish them well. He knew they had no idea about his gruesome deeds and activities. They would, of course, be shocked and amazed, if they knew the truth about their cousin, Michael.

At 10:00 a.m. Billy and Harry Trettin pulled up in a late model Chevrolet pick-up truck. Both men were honest, hard-working, blue-collar employees. Yet, they barely earned enough money to stay above water financially. The men lacked the intelligence, education, and drive it would take to get better paying jobs. And they didn't regret that, because they both loved working at the local saw mill, which was just outside of town. The men waved at him, when they recognized Michael sitting at a picnic table by himself studying the crowd of people at the picnic. He waved back and beckoned them to join him at the table. Billy brought brats and Harry had buns and burgers to cook. There were several grills located in the park. Harry shouldered his way up to one of the grills and placed six of Billy's brats on the grill. The two brothers slapped backs and joshed with other men gathered around the communal grill, while Michael watched with a bemused smile.

* * *

At noon, everyone gathered in the park stepped away from the grills and stopped their friendly chatter for a brief prayer offered by the local Presbyterian minister. As soon as the prayer was over, everyone made a bee-line toward two picnic tables where paper plates, utensils, paper napkins, and all kinds of assorted foods awaited. A separate table was set-up just for desserts. There was a smorgasbord of food and so much of it that no one would leave hungry. Bottled water was available for free and soft drinks were available for a small price to help cover the expenses of the event. A voluntary donation was requested by the event committee to help fund the next year's celebration.

After Michael and his cousins finished eating, they sat around reminiscing about their childhoods, relatives, and growing up in Higden. Naturally, Michael asked about his sister Emily Ann. Neither Billy nor Harry had any idea about her whereabouts, occupation, or family. Billy said that she might have passed away some years ago. He couldn't remember the source, but thought he'd heard that rumor from someone around town a while ago. Harry added, "Michael, I don't have any better news than what I told you the last time we talked. All I know is that I heard she lives or used to live somewhere around Branson, Missouri. But who knows for sure."

"Well, if you ever hear anything about her, please let me know. I'd like to know one way or another," Michael replied.

"We'll be sure to let you know, if we ever hear anything, Michael," Billy said nodding his head sincerely.

"Yup, sure will," Harry added and patted Smith on the shoulder.

"I know you will, and that's one of the reasons why I appreciate talking to you guys. But how are you two doing, really? How's life after divorce?"

Billy replied first. "I still see the kids, but my ex-wife has a boyfriend and thankfully she doesn't bother me much, as long as she gets her check," Billy said sounding relieved.

"How about you Harry, is that bitch still harassing you?"

"Well, I have joint custody of the boy and things are alright. I need to see my lawyer to find out if I can take her back to court for more child support. For a while, she wasn't paying me anything. My lawyer says if she starts missing payments again, she might go to jail and the court could give me full custody rights. That would be fine with me," Harry said with emphasis. "The boy and I love each other and we're good friends too. We treat each other well and are respectful to each other."

"How about you, Michael, are you ever gonna get hitched?" asked Billy.

"I have a few lady-friends back in Florida, but I don't feel the need to get married right now. Maybe someday. My physical needs are being met by a couple different women I like. But I don't believe either of them wants to get married again. Both were involved in unhappy relationships and I think they're not interested in taking another chance, at least not any time soon." Smith chuckled. "But you know how a woman can be. Their attitudes can change one-hundred eighty degrees without warning."

His two cousins both laughed ruefully, and then said in unison, "That's fer damn sure!"

"I was told by a family friend that he saw my wife out flirtin', kissin', and gropin' men at different bars in Clinton," Harry blurted out. "And it wasn't the first time I heard that news," he said sadly shaking his head. "If you didn't know better, you'd think she was a whore."

"Did you ever catch her cheating on you?" Michael asked earnestly.

"No, but I used to wonder if she had something going on at times."

"If she'd been my wife, I'd have followed her and found out the truth," Michael said through clenched teeth.

"Maybe I should have, but what good would that do me now?" Harry asked.

"If it was me, I'd like to know for my own piece of mind," Michael replied, still gritting his teeth." *And I know what I'd do to her. It would be the last time she'd do that.*

"I don't give a crap what she does anymore. I'll never take her back and I don't think she wants to come back to me either," Harry said dismissively. "Would you ever consider taking your wife back, Billy?" asked Harry seriously.

"Hell no, brother! I had enough of her and marriage to last a lifetime."

"What do you boys do for entertainment these days?" inquired Michael changing the subject.

"Aren't you busy enough with your clients and your own projects at home?" questioned Harry.

"Yeah, but sometimes it's nice to do something different for a weekend. If you don't boat or fish, Higden doesn't have much to offer. I might be interested in making a new friend or two in Arkansas. After all, it's several more months before I head back to Florida," Michael noted with a sly smile. "You know I get lonely sometimes," he added intimately. "Where do you two go to meet women?"

"I haven't been to Little Rock for a while, but there are plenty of horny women there," Billy said. "Just go to any local bar. There are usually all kinds of women ready to hop into the sack for the night. That is, if all you want is to get lucky, Cousin. But sometimes there's a price for their companionship," Billy added with a chuckle and slapped Smith on the shoulder.

"I've been thinking about it lately. I'm really not interested in getting serious. Just looking for a one-night stand," Michael said and then winked at Billy.

"Well, Little Rock is the place for you," said Harry smiling.

Michael thought for a moment and said, "You might be right. I met a waitress in Little Rock one time. She was my type physically, but I think she was religious."

"Speaking of needs, Cousin, you know religious girls have needs too. You'd be surprised how horny they can be under the right circumstances," chuckled Harry.

"Are you speaking from experience, Harry?" Michael asked lasciviously.

"Yeah, it was a long time ago, but right here in Higden. You wouldn't believe it, if I told you," Harry said with a satisfied smile spreading across his face with the recollection.

"Sure, I would, but you can keep your secrets, Harry. I understand," Michael replied frankly. "I know it's none of my business. We all keep secrets about ourselves, don't we?"

"Yes, we do!" the cousins replied in unison.

"Michael, do you ever regret leaving Arkansas and relocating in Florida?" Billy asked.

"I'll tell you this. I liked Arkansas well enough, but my mother made it almost impossible for me to stay here. You know how she was. It got so bad in the end; I didn't think I had much of a choice. For the most part, Florida has been good. I like the weather there, but I miss the people in Arkansas. People here are more relaxed and they're friendlier than the people I've met in Florida."

"Yeah, I remember what your childhood was like. At least my parents stayed together long enough and seemed happy, until we were out of the house," Billy said looking off into the distance.

"Hey, let's go get some dessert. I forgot about it once we got to talking." Michael wanted to divert their attention away from talking about his childhood. It was always an uncomfortable subject for him to discuss, even with relatives. If they only knew half of what he and Emily Ann had endured, there would never be any questions about his childhood, Michael thought.

"Good idea!" Harry affirmed. The three men headed over to the dessert table.

After they polished off their desserts, Harry, Billy, and Michael walked to the parking lot together. Before the brothers said their goodbyes to Michael, it was agreed they'd meet the following day to pay their respects to their departed relatives at the graveyard.

Chapter 13

Two weeks after the Home Coming and Decoration Day weekend, Smith decided to go to Branson, Missouri, for a brief get-away. He planned to attend a country music show and look for another victim. The increased pressure by the authorities to capture him had shaken Smith, but it also awakened his desire to find and murder another whore. Seven weeks had passed since he murdered the young harlot in the Chicot County pine forest. He was more than ready for the next.

Instead of heading to Little Rock, Arkansas for some "paid companionship", as suggested by his cousins, Smith decided to go north to Branson, Missouri. If he couldn't find a suitable victim in Branson, at least he would enjoy the musical entertainment on "The Strip" along Highway 76. He liked country music and had been to the Grand Country Music Hall, Presley's Country Jubilee, and even Dick Clark's American Bandstand Theatre.

Most of the shows were good and the performers knew how to please their audiences. At the conclusion of the shows most of the musicians held "meet and greets" to sign autographs for the fans. Articles of clothing and other collectibles could be purchased for a nominal fee along with CD's and albums of the performing musicians.

Most of the theaters sold matinee tickets for Saturday afternoon performances. After watching a matinee, Smith planned to eat and then pick out his next victim at one of several local Branson bars. Although Branson is known for its family-oriented entertainment, there are always some loose women available for a price.

The first thing Smith planned to do once he arrived in Branson was to check into a cheap motel room in one of the shadier roadside locations near the outskirts of town. He knew from experience that a low-end highway motel was less likely to have security cameras on the premises than the more well-known motel chains. Clerks manning the front desks of shadier motels were typically under-educated, under-paid, and part-time employees. They were the type that asked few questions and could care less about what their customers were doing in the rooms. Their mission was to collect the room charges and call the cops if their temporary residents got too rowdy or out of control. Smith always paid in advance with cash. Usually, he'd ask for an end room near the back of the motel complex and park his car around the corner from the room.

Smith arrived in Branson, Missouri around 11:00 a.m. after driving three hours from Higden, Arkansas. He quickly found a dumpy motel where he secured a room. The front desk clerk asked to see his driver's license at check-in and for the make, model, and license plate number of his vehicle. He showed the clerk a fake license and provided misinformation concerning the vehicle. As usual, the clerk didn't bother to check the accuracy of the vehicle information. Once inside the room, Smith decided to take a short nap, soak in a warm tub, and prepare himself for the day's events.

Smith left the motel in time for the 2:00 p.m. matinee. He drove his Toyota to the Presleys' Country Jubilee Theatre, which was several miles from the motel. He parked as close to the front door as possible in the theater's parking lot and walked into the lobby. Smith purchased a ticket for a seat near the back of the theatre. The show lasted two-hours.

Smith left the theater to look for a restaurant that served reasonably priced food. It was 5 p.m. when he walked out of the restaurant. He decided to drive around the strip and do some sightseeing before beginning the search for his next victim. He tentatively planned to check out the Foot Hill's Club and Grill as the first stop in the search for the type of woman he wanted to kill. Smith had struck up a conversation with a local he'd met at the restaurant where he'd eaten dinner. The dude told him that the best selection of available women in Branson on a Saturday night was at the Foot Hill's Club and Grill. He said women usually started arriving at the club around 8:00.

Smith did not want to be too familiar with a bar's staff, so his modus operandi was to wait outside in his vehicle and watch for women to begin arriving for the evening. The type of woman he was looking for would be fairly attractive, wearing heavy makeup, smelling of inexpensive perfume, and wearing revealing clothing. Inside, she would be sitting alone on a bar stool drinking a cocktail. A woman scanning the room for men or flirting with them was immediately on Smith's radar. His usual routine was to sit down next to a woman that fit the desired profile and offer to buy her a drink. At first, there would be some superficial conversation and they'd have a drink. Before too long, the type of woman he was looking for would begin to make suggestive remarks. She would slyly hint about whether he'd like to have a date with her. If she was a prostitute or just a whore on the make, she would soon be suggesting that they leave separately and meet in his car.

He appreciated the superior caliber of women willing to provide sexual favors for free or for cash in Branson. He knew the women here were older, more discrete and experienced, unlike his normal choice of younger, prettier, and more vulnerable women to choose from in other locales.

Smith would never drug a victim at a bar during the pick-up stage. He waited until they were alone in a motel room. If possible, it was better to use her motel room for sex. Most of the older and more experienced hookers had their own rooms close to the bars they frequented. They wanted to get the sex over quickly so they could return to the club or street to pick up another John.

There were women at the clubs just looking for companionship and the thrill of experiencing a one-night-stand. They appealed to Smith too. In his mind, the only difference between the two was whether or not they charged for sex. Both types were whores and didn't deserve to live.

At 8:30 p.m., while watching from his minivan in the

club's parking lot, Smith noticed a short, thin, mature woman with dish-water blond hair getting out of a taxi. She instantly reminded him of his mother. The woman was probably in her mid-forties. Her black dress was simple but sexy. Smith noticed her glossy-black, high heel shoes and nicely formed legs. He wondered if she worked out at a local gym as he followed her into the Foot Hills Club and Grill. She spotted an empty stool near the end of the bar and sat down. The bartender quickly came over to her and they exchanged pleasantries. Smith figured she was one of the Saturday night regulars.

When she pulled out a cigarette, Smith immediately appeared and lit it for her. She quickly looked him over and said, "Thank you." She favored him with a friendly smile.

"Thanking me is not necessary. I saw you needed a light and I responded as any gentleman would," he said suavely. "Can I join you and buy your next drink?" Smith asked politely, but with a slight gleam in his eye.

"I'd like that very much," she said while raising her left eye brow and letting an alluring grin spread across her face.

Smith casually took a seat next to her at the bar and said, "Are you here on vacation or are you from Branson?"

"I live in Springfield, Missouri, but I like to come see the shows on weekends. Where are you from?" she asked with a sexy drawl.

"I'm just passing through Branson," Smith replied as he turned towards her on the bar stool to get a closer look at her. "I've never been here before but I like country music. I went to a matinee this afternoon."

"Was it good?" she asked.

"Yes, very."

"I'm Erica." Her eyes drift over Smith's physical features. Extending her hand, she sweetly said, "Nice to meet you."

Smith shook her hand gently and said softly, "I'm Paul Stuart. It's very nice to meet you, Erica."

"What brings you to Branson, business or pleasure?"

"I sell air tools to the automobile industry. I'm on my way to St. Louis. I have an appointment with the production manager of the Chrysler plant this coming Monday. However, I'm free all weekend," he said with a sly smile.

"What a coincidence. I don't have to be back in Springfield until Monday either."

"Are you ready for another drink?" Smith asked casually.

"Yes, thank you Paul, I am. Just tell the bartender I want another drink. He knows what I like." Erica stepped off the bar stool and using an intimate tone said, "I'll be right back, don't you go away." She headed toward the restroom, but slowly stopped, turned, and gave him a sexy smile and a wink.

Upon her return to the bar, she noticed a partially filled glass of red wine sitting in front of her seat. "The bartender said you like Pinot Noir," Smith said.

"I really do," she said smiling at him.

"I selected a very nice Pinot Noir for you from the MacMurray Estate Vineyards. It's a California wine. I hope you enjoy it. But, if you don't like it, say so. I'll drink it myself and get you something else."

"I'm sure it will be perfectly fine," she said appreciatively. "After we have our drink would you like to go somewhere else that has a more romantic atmosphere?" Erica asked boldly while throwing back her shoulders, so her breasts pushed against the fabric of her dress.

Smith was pleased with how well the liaison was developing. It was proceeding even more quickly than he had expected. Erica had apparently splashed on a bit of perfume while she was in the restroom for his enjoyment. It had a pleasing aroma. "What do you have in mind?" Smith intended to sound interested, but he also tried to express a little naivety in his tone.

"Just trust me," she told him as she softly touched his arm and began to lightly caress his shoulder. "Do you have a car here?" Erica asked nonchalantly.

"Yes, I do." Smith was careful not to sound too eager. He wanted Erica to think she was in charge of what was happening between them.

"Great!" she replied enthusiastically. "I'll meet you outside in a few minutes. Just wait for me in your car. I need to make a telephone call before I can leave." She gave him a bright smile and squeezed his arm.

Smith returned her smile, but tried to look a little shy. As he walked out of the club, he wondered whether she was calling a husband or a boyfriend to make an excuse for being late for some other engagement.

Several minutes later Erica emerged from the club and waved when she saw him sitting in his Toyota at the curb outside the front door of the bar. She quickly got in and said straight out, "I want us to be together tonight. Do you have a motel room?"

"No, I'm staying with friends," Smith lied but stuttered slightly as if surprised at her suggestion.

"That's fine," Erica said calmly. "I have one."

Traffic was heavy, but ten minutes later they pulled into a modestly priced motel. Erica instructed him to park his minivan in the side lot. "My room is in the back, around the corner," she said.

The thought that this might be a set up flashed through Smith's mind. Was he about to be mugged? *No, she's not the criminal type.* But, before he completely dismissed the possibility, he asked in an innocent-sounding tone, "Who did you call back at the bar?"

"Just my girlfriend. I told her I'd meet her later for a cocktail, but it looks like I'm going to be busy for the night," Erica said smiling while looking deep into his eyes.

"Did she come with you from Springfield?"

"No, she's from Branson. We'd planned to meet for a drink at the Foothills Club at 9:30. But I don't think I'm going to be available," she said with a sexy shrug of her shoulders while flipping her hair to the side.

"You still can," Smith replied with an affected tone of sincerity in his voice.

Erica giggled and then said, "No, my dear. I will meet her tomorrow night. Because tonight," she said as she put her arms around him and pulled him close, "I'm going to be with you." Then she kissed him long and hard on the lips.

He returned her passionate kiss and worked his tongue slowly into her open mouth. Smith could feel her body quivering and he sensed the passion she was about to unleash. When they entered the motel room, Smith immediately noticed her opened suitcase lying on the queen-sized bed nearest the door. He also noticed that there was an unopened bottle of red wine sitting on the dresser. "Would you like a glass of wine to help you relax?" Smith asked helpfully pointing at the bottle.

"Sure, that would be nice. Please go ahead and pour us each a glass of wine. I'll be right back. But first, I need to change into something more comfortable." There was a tremble of excitement in her voice.

"I'd be happy too, Erica," he said smiling at her.

"Please leave my drink on the nightstand, take off your clothes, and get into bed," she instructed him from inside the bathroom. We'll have a toast before we go to bed," she said sweetly.

Smith chuckled to himself coldheartedly. He realized his next victim was a lonely woman looking for companionship and sex. At first, he thought she was a prostitute, but turns out she is just a horny woman looking for men to pick-up at a club. Smith wondered if she was unhappily married and was out cheating on her husband. He had noted she was not wearing a wedding ring; not that it mattered. Hastily, he poured an adequate dose of his date-rape drug into her drink and stirred it with his finger. He removed his clothing, placed her drink on the night stand, got into bed, and left the table light on for her.

When she returned, Smith offered a toast, "To our new friendship."

She sat on the side of the bed while they sipped the wine and made casual conversation. After a few minutes, Smith encouraged her to finish the drink. She obediently drained the glass, hiccupped, and then giggled. Erica reached out to turn off the lamp, which allowed her negligee to slip low enough to reveal her cleavage. Smith smiled and nodded appreciatively. Erica stood and let her negligee slip off. Then, she pulled the covers up and returned his appreciative smile while surveying his naked body.

In bed, he immediately embraced her and began kissing and caressing her. He wanted her to think they would be making love just like any horny couple on a first date. Yet, he couldn't help wondering how long it would take for the drug to kick in. His need to move to the next phase was building.

Erica noticed that his initial gentleness had given way to a more hurried and aggressive approach to love-making. Erica liked aggressive men, but she was beginning to wonder if Paul wasn't as shy and gentlemanly as he first seemed. When he began to thrust into her, it was beyond aggressive. It felt vicious. But just as she started to protest and ask him to slow down and be gentler, she felt very light-headed. How much wine have I drunk? A minute later, she passed out.

Smith stared at the naked and unconscious woman. He had planned to start strangling her before she passed out. This would have to be a fairly quick kill, he decided. Still, the anticipation of killing her excited him. The feeling of power, dominance, and strength made him believe that, at least for a time, he was super human. By killing her he was able to defy the laws of nature and God. He knew he was special. Who but a few other men were capable of doing what he did?

Smith smiled savagely as he quickly dressed and then went outside to his minivan. He returned to the motel room with his bucket of tools. He couldn't afford to wait several hours for Erica to wake up to perform his normal ritual. Oh well, a quick kill was better than nothing, Smith thought wickedly as he prepared his tool kit.

Smith repeatedly raped Erica's lifeless body until he felt physically spent. He briefly contemplated how he would perform the next phase. Instead of choking her to death, Smith decided to use his hunting knife to carver her up. At the very least, it would be pleasurable to cut her up a bit before finishing her off.

The bed was soaked with blood when he was done. He admired his work and felt pleased. Smith took a quick shower, cleaned off the knife, and hastily covered her body with the bed spread. Next, he carefully rubbed out his foot prints on the carpet and cleaned up the bathroom floor. He removed his finger prints from the room, put on his clothes, and then took Polaroid photographs of his victim. He placed the photos and the negatives inside a small manila envelope.

Smith rifled through Erica's purse. He found her car keys, a wallet, miscellaneous personal items, and identification documents. Smith dumped the purse and its contents, minus the cash and credit cards, into a dumpster at the back of the motel parking lot. He intended to make the crime scene look like a break-in, rape, robbery, and a murder. He thought the M.O. was sufficiently different from his style, that the authorities would not connect it to the murder in Chicot County or any of his other serial murders.

Before leaving, he used a crow bar to pull off the security chain from the door casing. Then, he jammed a flat-head screwdriver into the door lock breaking the lock, so it would look like there had been a break-in. Smith carried his tool bucket along with the glass, the wine bottle, the condom he'd used, and the manila envelope containing the photos back to his vehicle. He planned to dispose of the glass, bottle, and the condom either at a fast food restaurant or in a gas station trash container.

On the way to the club to begin his hunt that evening, Smith had filled his gas tank. Following the kill, he drove back to his motel, removed his finger prints from the room, packed his bag, and left the key inside on the dresser. There was no need to check-out, since he had prepaid in cash. The three-hour trip back to Higden was uneventful.

He assumed one of the women who worked in house-keeping at the motel would find Erica's body sometime the following day. Smith was not too concerned. No one could link the two of them together except for the brief time he had spent with her inside the Foot Hill's Club and Grill. He doubted that the bartender would even remember his face. Smith had worn glasses and had partially dyed his hair grey. He had worn casual clothing and looked like an ordinary guy in a bar having a drink. Erica thought she was going out with Paul Stuart. If she mentioned her liaison's name to the friend she had telephoned from the bar, that would be the guy's name. He didn't think anyone knew him or could ID him in Branson. As he drove back to Higden, he smiled with satisfaction that he had covered his tracks well. He felt confident that anything about the crime that could lead the authorities to him had been taken care of.

What Smith didn't know was that there was a witness outside the club, who had seen him leave with Erica. The witness, however, did not know who Smith was. What he knew was that he had seen his ex-wife getting into a dark-colored Toyota minivan. The plate number was not visible, because Smith had placed the plate inside the back window so it was hard to see. After all, it was just a temporary paper plate.

The witness was Erica's ex-husband, Phillip Danforth, who had been tipped off to his ex-wife's presence at the club by her girlfriend. The girlfriend liked Phillip and had agreed to help him get Erica back. Phillip followed the Toyota as it pulled away from the club. But traffic was heavy and he soon lost sight of the Toyota somewhere on

Highway 76. Phillip searched for a half-hour trying to locate the vehicle, but he eventually stopped looking and headed home.

Phillip's purpose at the club was to see if Erica was currently involved with another man. If so, he wanted to talk to her about whether there was any hope of getting back together or had she fallen in love with someone else. He was still confused about what had caused their marriage to end. Erica's girlfriend had assured him there was no one else, while they were married, but he was not sure whether he could believe her or not. After seeing her get into a vehicle with another man, he wondered if his suspicions had been correct. Admittedly, he didn't know whether she'd been involved with this guy while they were still married. It pained him either way, but based on what he could observe from a distance at the club, and his wish to believe Erica had not been unfaithful while they were married, Phillip thought it looked as if Erica's liaison was only a one-night-stand with the driver of the Toyota.

Luckily for Phillip, he didn't meet up with Smith that evening. If he had, Michael James Smith probably would have panicked and killed them both. Erica was not so lucky. She was horny and had decided Paul Stuart was going to be the recipient of her sexual favors for the evening. Erica had allowed herself to be charmed by a ruthless, sadistic monster. By the time she realized there was something seriously wrong with Stuart, it was too late.

Chapter 14

Maddy Jackson cleaned rooms at the Top Rate Motel and Suites. For twenty years she'd been slow but diligent at housekeeping for the motel. Maddy's complexion was coal black and she was 100-pounds overweight. She was very religious and liked to hum and quietly sing her favorite hymns while she cleaned rooms at the Top Rate.

Room 189, registered to Erica Danforth, was the last room on Maddy's list for the day. She pushed her cleaning cart up to the door, knocked, and called out, "Housekeeping!" Maddy stopped humming *Amazing Grace* and waited for a response. Since there was no reply, Maddy reached into her pocket for the master key to unlock the door. But then, she noticed the lock was damaged. *Good gracious! Somebody's been messin' with this lock. Uh huh.*

Maddy knocked on the door again and this time shouted, "Housekeeping!" She knocked once more and then tried to use the master key to open the door. The key didn't work, but when she turned the door handle and pushed on the door it opened. Maddy immediately smelled a foul, repulsive odor inside the room. She started to mutter about guests leaving food out to rot, but quickly realized the stench was the worst she'd ever encountered in one of the Top Rate's rooms.

Maddy glanced around the room and pinched her nose as she entered. The motel room appeared normal with the exception that there was an open suitcase lying on the undisturbed queen-size bed. It wasn't the first time a guest left belongings behind after check-out time. Looking at her wrist watch, Maddy noted it was almost 1:00 p.m., two hours past the 11:00 a.m. check-out time. The second bed looked like it had been slept in. The bed spread was sloppily thrown over the bed and it looked lumpy, like there was something underneath the covers. The bathroom door was closed.

After twenty years in housekeeping at a highway motel, not much surprised Maddy. And so far, she wasn't surprised about the state of Room 189. However, her sixth sense told her that there was something wrong inside this room.

She cautiously stepped forward and asked in a nervous voice, "Is anyone here? I's with Housekeeping." Still no response. As Maddy walked past the closest bed she pulled up short. There were spots of blood on the tan carpet, on the mattress, and on the white sheet that was dangling over the side of the second bed. Her mind began to fill with dread. *What in the Good Lord's name happened here?*

Maddy slowly pulled back the bed spread. There was more blood and then, "Oh dear Lord!" she shrieked. A naked, decomposing female-body was under the bed spread.

Maddy ran out of the room screaming, "Help! Help! Help!"

Oliva, the maid at the other end of the hall heard Maddy's scream and began running toward the screams.

"What's wrong, Maddy?" Oliva asked panting as she reached the older woman. "What you screamin' help for?"

"Dear God!" Maddy cried, gulping deep breaths and shaking. "There's a dead body in Room 189 an' it looks like she been cut up and murdered! Go get dat manager! Quick now, girl!" Maddy was sobbing hysterically.

"Get holda yerself, Maddy! I'll be right back with Mr. Spencer." Oliva turned on her heel and scampering off toward the office. "He'll know what to do," she called back hopefully.

A few minutes later Oliva and Jack Spencer, the day manager, were trotting around the back of the motel to Room 189. They were out of breath, when Spencer gasped, "Are you alright, Maddy?"

"God almighty, Mr. Spencer! I never seen nothin' like this in all my born days. I need to sit down or I'm gonna pass out."

"Olivia, take Maddy to the next room and help her lie down, please," Spencer said in a calming voice. "Stay with her until the police and the EMTs arrive. The EMTs can check her out. I'm sure the police will want to interview her."

"Yes sir, Mr. Spencer. I'll take good care of her." Oliva put her arm around Maddy's plump shoulder and gently tugged her into the room next door.

"That's good, very good, thank you," Spencer called after the one large and second slight figure retreating into the adjacent room. "My god, I hope she doesn't have a heart attack," Spencer muttered to himself.

Before the authorities arrived, Spencer stuck his head inside Room 189. The smell was dreadful and he almost vomited when he saw the woman's decomposing body on the bed.

* * *

Ten minutes later the Top Rate Motel was crawling with law enforcement personnel from the Branson Police Department and the Taney County Sheriff's Department. The Branson Chief of Police directed officers to tape off the crime scene and secure the area. The local coroner was called to inspect the body and try to calculate the time of death. Spencer informed the police that the victim had checked into the motel the previous afternoon. The Taney County detectives were assigned to help gather information about the victim. The Branson Police Chief notified the Missouri State Police and requested the State Police to send their criminal investigative unit to Branson from St. Louis. They were expected to arrive within several hours.

EMT's arrived and evaluated Maddy Jackson to determine whether she should be seen by a physician. By the time the EMT's arrived, Maddy had calmed down.

After questioning and examining her, the EMT's decided she would be alright. Mr. Spencer sent her home.

The Taney County Sheriff deputies discovered the victim's purse in a dumpster at the far end of the motel parking lot. Identification papers found inside the purse revealed that the victim was Erica J. Danforth from Springfield, Missouri. That information was consistent with the information provided to the clerk at check-in. No credit cards or cash were found in the wallet inside the purse. A white, Buick Rendezvous SUV registered to Ms. Danforth was located in the motel parking lot in a space near her room. The Branson police photographer photographed the crime scene and the victim. The Sheriff's department chief investigator dusted and took fingerprint impressions from every surface inside the room and on the door.

After an initial review of the evidence and consultation with the local authorities the Missouri State Police officials determined the killing was more than just a routine homicide. A call was made to the FBI for assistance.

* * *

Around 4:00 p.m. EST, Giordano took a telephone call at Quantico from the Missouri FBI field office. He recorded the details provided. Giordano filled Larcovic in on the developments in Missouri. They both wondered whether the homicide in Branson was committed by the same serial killer they were hunting for the murder in

Chicot County, Arkansas. Ten minutes later, Larcovic was in Director Underwood's office. After listening to Larcovic's report, Underwood authorized a two-man team to investigate the crime.

Bouldon and Giordano were instructed by Larcovic to catch the next flight to St. Louis, where they would be met by Jonathon Anderson, the local FBI field agent. Anderson was charged with meeting them at the St. Louis Lambert International Airport and then to drive the agents to Branson. He would help coordinate with the local authorities involved in the investigation. Before Bouldon and Giordano departed the office, Larcovic ordered Bouldon to provide him a preliminary report on the following morning.

* * *

The agents arrived in St. Louis at 8:30 p.m. CST. As expected, Anderson was awaiting their arrival and immediately drove them to the Top Rate Motel in Branson, arriving at 11:00 p.m. Anderson introduced the two BSU special agents to the police officers standing guard at the crime scene. They learned from the local officers that the body had been examined by a Missouri State homicide forensics expert and had been moved to the local morgue several hours earlier.

It was almost midnight when agents Bouldon, Giordano, and Anderson each ordered a piece of pie and coffee at the roadside restaurant across the street from the motel. After they finished their late-night snack, the three agents checked into separate rooms at the Top Rate for the night. It had been a long day and they were tired. Still, neither Bouldon nor Giordano drifted off easily into sleep. They were both excited and anxious to start the next phase of the investigation in the morning.

* * *

As agreed, Bouldon, Giordano, and Anderson were up and out of bed at 7:00 a.m. They walked across the road to the diner, ate a quick breakfast and proceeded to the back of the motel to inspect the crime scene. The State Police team, by agreement with the Branson Police Chief, was in charge of the investigation. The lead officer with the State Police was scheduled to review the evidence with the FBI team at 8:00 a.m. The meeting was held in a temporary command post set up in another room at the motel. The detective in charge of the case was Sergeant Robert H. Whitcomb of the Missouri State Police.

Agent Anderson, who knew Whitcomb from previous cases they'd worked, introduced Bouldon and Giordano as members of the FBI Behavioral Science Unit. Bouldon explained their interest in the case was based on the similarities to a recent murder case they were working on in Arkansas. Pleasantries were exchanged and then the men got down to the business of working through the available information on the current murder case in Branson.

The FBI agents learned from Sergeant Whitcomb that

the body of a Caucasian woman in her late 40's was found in her motel room on Sunday around 1:00 p.m. by one of the motel's maids. The Sergeant stated the victim had been killed in Room 189 and was left on top of the bed in the motel room. The killer had hastily covered the corpse with the bed spread prior to leaving. The coroner set the time of death between 9:00 p.m. and 10:00 p.m. on Saturday night. The autopsy revealed she had been stabbed several times in the chest and had died as a result of those injuries. There was a sexy negligee found next to the bed, along with an empty glass on the night stand. A red-colored residue remained in the bottom of the glass and the forensics expert believed it was wine. The glass was at the lab in St. Louis being evaluated. To determine whether the victim had engaged in intercourse prior to the murder, the Coroner and the State Police forensics expert had examined her vaginal area. They determined that recent penetration had occurred and speculated that the victim was probably raped prior to her death. Three stab wounds in her chest were about five inches in depth and the murder weapon was believed to be a large knife with a serrated blade.

"What is the victim's full name and what background information is known about her?" Giordano asked as he scribbled on a legal pad.

"The victim's name is Erica J. Danforth. She's a natural blond, 47-years old, and kind of a looker," Whitcomb said with an arched brow. "She has been divorced for almost a year. Ms. Danforth and her ex-husband are currently living apart in Springfield, Missouri. She is a local real estate agent and her former husband, Mr. Phillip Danforth, is an advertising executive for a major national firm. They have no children and the divorce was amicably settled, according to Mr. Danforth. However, he also states that his wife had lost interest in their relationship and he suspected her of having a boyfriend. So that casts some doubt on how amicable the divorce was," Whitcomb concluded arching his brow again.

"Well, she apparently did have someone," Bouldon commented dispassionately in his distinct Creole accent. "Did you interview the person who found the body?"

"Yes, shortly after we arrived on the scene, we talked to a Ms. Maddy Jackson. She discovered the body in the room."

"What did she have to say, if anything?" Bouldon asked somewhat querulously.

"We asked her to tell us if she noticed anything missing in the room," Sgt. Whitcomb replied placidly.

"And, was there anything missing?" Bouldon asked peremptorily.

"Yes, she stated there were supposed to be two water glasses in the room and the investigators only found one with the victim's fingerprints all over it."

"Were there any other fingerprints or DNA evidence found at the crime scene?" Giordano asked.

"Yes, lots of them, from the victim," Whitcomb replied. He shook his head dejectedly. "Our detectives checked for fingerprints and DNA from the killer, but unfortunately, he must have wiped the room clean before leaving. There were fingerprints from the victim everywhere and her hair follicles were found in the bathroom too, but nothing else. Also, we believe the killer took a shower after the murder and the towel he used to dry himself off is being examined for DNA evidence. We think he cleaned up the bathroom too before departing."

"Did your team check for skin or hair samples in the shower drain?" Giordano asked.

"As a matter of fact, they did, but a strong acid had been dumped down the drain to destroy any traces of DNA. However, we do hope to find some skin samples and possibly hair from the killer and the deceased in the bed sheets," Whitcomb stated brightly.

"Did you find anything else that might help to identify the assailant?" Bouldon asked unemotionally.

"I'm sorry. Unfortunately, as of now, we don't have many leads." Detective Whitcomb said looking disappointed.

The two BSU agents continued their questioning of Whitcomb trying to squeeze every bit of relevant information from him. He explained that the State Police and Sheriff's detectives had already begun to piece together a time-line of Ms. Danforth's last hours.

"Our time-line begins the previous Saturday at 12:30 p.m. when a Springfield, Missouri neighbor saw Ms. Danforth's Buick pull out of the driveway. The neighbor, an older lady, stated that she had not seen her since then." Whitcomb continued, "According to a close friend of Ms. Danforth, who lives in the Branson area, Ms. Danforth called her earlier in the day to arrange a meeting for the two of them on Saturday night. They were to meet at 9:30 p.m. in Branson at the Foot Hills Club and Grill for a drink. However, just before 9:00 p.m. Ms. Danforth called her friend to postpone the meeting until the following night, claiming she had met someone and would be tied up for the evening."

"Did the friend say Ms. Danforth had disclosed who she met?" Giordano asked.

"She did not. Ms. Danforth was last seen alive in the Foot Hill's Club and Grill at 9:00 p.m. by the bartender. He says Ms. Danforth was sitting at the bar drinking a glass of wine. Several minutes later, he noticed an unknown man sitting next to her at the bar. The man bought her a drink and shortly thereafter the bartender noticed Ms. Danforth was gone. Several minutes later, he noticed the man had departed the bar as well. The bartender assumed they left together to go somewhere else."

"Interesting," Bouldon remarked. "Did the bartender remember what the man looked like?" Bouldon asked excitedly.

"Yes, he described the man as being in his mid-forties, having dark-brown graying hair, wearing glasses, medium build, and casually dressed. The bartender claimed he'd never seen the man before, but recognized Ms. Danforth. She'd become somewhat of a regular at the club."

"Alright!" Bouldon exclaimed. "That's the kind of stuff I want to hear. I assume he gave you a statement and a police artist made a sketch of the suspect's face?"

"Yes, I'll make sure you get a copy of the statement and

the drawing," Sergeant Whitcomb said.

"Good, thank you. That will be great," Bouldon said enthusiastically.

Giordano interjected, "Did the bartender say the man had a beard or a goatee?"

"No, according to the bartender, he was clean shaven," Whitcomb said shaking his head. "There's more, but I'll refer you to his statement."

"Thank you, I'll study the statement with the rest of your case file on the airplane ride back to Quantico," Giordano said.

"Fortunately, there is another witness," Whitcomb proclaimed proudly. "But strangely, it's her ex-husband, Mr. Phillip Danforth. He claims to have seen his ex-wife leave the club a little after 9:00 p.m. in a dark-colored 2000 Toyota Sienna. The driver of the Toyota and the license plate on the vehicle were not seen by Mr. Danforth."

"What was Mr. Danforth supposedly doing at the bar?" Agent Bouldon asked in astonishment.

"He claims he was following his ex-wife to see if she was meeting another man," Whitcomb replied with his now characteristic arched brow.

"That's a flimsy sounding excuse, don't you think?" Bouldon said, his own brow arched skeptically.

"I agree, but we interviewed him extensively and we don't believe he had anything to do with the murder. His statement is in the file I'll give you."

"Why is he not a suspect?" Agent Bouldon blurted out. "The husband, or the ex-husband in this case, they are usually the primary suspects in this type of murder. Don't you agree, Sergeant?" Bouldon demanded.

"Well, because everything he told us checked out," Whitcomb said with open palms. "You can interview him yourself, if you like. Just so you'll know, I've been doing this stuff for almost twenty years and I'll bet my bottom dollar he's not a killer."

"How did he respond when you told him about his ex-wife?" Bouldon asked coolly.

"Naturally, he was very upset following the revelation of his ex-wife being found murdered. He wept for quite a while before calming down cnough to allow us to take a statement. In an effort to clear himself as a suspect, he even offered to take a polygraph test - which he passed with flying colors," Sergeant Whitcomb said meeting Bouldon's skeptical gaze.

"You know polygraphs aren't admissible in court for a reason, right Sergeant?" Bouldon replied in a patronizing tone. "Surely you know of suspects who defeated the test."

"I don't think Mr. Danforth's personality warrants further suspicion," Whitcomb replied emphatically. "Look, to put it plainly, Mr. Danforth is a bona fide wimp. When I first met him, I thought he was gay. But whether he is or isn't, doesn't matter. He's just not the type to do such a terrible thing to any woman, let alone his ex-wife."

"Don't kid yourself, Whitcomb, anything is possible when feelings are involved," Bouldon insisted.

"His ex-wife's friend told us she was trying to help Phillip out because he still was in love with her and wanted them to get back together," Whitcomb said defensively.

"What did he say when he found out she was with another man?" Bouldon pressed.

"Mr. Danforth said he didn't blame her for wanting companionship. After all, he pointed out that they were divorced. She was free to do what she wanted and he stated if they got back together, those things would be forgiven."

"Well, for the moment, I'm going to consider him as a serious suspect regardless of what he has said or done. I'd like to have his name and address just in case we want to interview him after we've reviewed the file," Bouldon said insistently.

"I'll be happy to provide that information to you today, before you leave," Detective Whitcomb assured him in a placating tone.

"Thank you, Sergeant," Bouldon said and shrugged his shoulders.

"Oh, I forgot something," Whitcomb said and tapped his forehead. "According to Mr. Danforth, he tried to follow the Toyota. But the traffic was heavy, as usual, on a Saturday night. He lost them several blocks later."

"Too bad he couldn't keep up with them in traffic," Bouldon commented dryly, still wondering whether Danforth had been truthful about anything. For all they knew, he thought, *Danforth could have hired a hit man to kill his ex-wife because he couldn't do it himself. Maybe he made up the entire story about seeing her driving away from the bar in a Toyota SUV. He could be trying to send the investigation off in a wild goose chase to cover his ass.*

Sergeant Whitcomb next showed the FBI agents a security camera video tape recording made at the Top Rate Motel at about 9:15 p.m. It showed a dark-colored Toyota Sienna pulling into the parking lot of the motel. "As you can see, there were two people in the vehicle. Around 10:30 p.m. you see the same Toyota leaving the motel. But now, there is only a driver in the front seat of the vehicle," Whitcomb stated.

"Are there any witnesses that can identify or describe the driver of the Toyota?" Bouldon asked Sergeant Whitcomb hoping for a positive response.

"No, Mr. Danforth claims he never saw the driver of the Toyota. As you can see, the quality of the video tape is pretty bad. The motel reuses old and worn-out tapes, so it's not much help. We've had the local police officers review the tape to see whether any of them could make a positive ID, but it's too grainy."

Giordano grunted with disgust. *What was the point of making a security tape recording, if the tape used was in such crappy condition it was basically worthless!* He had hoped Mr. Danforth had identified the vehicle as being a 1999 Dodge Caravan. *If the vehicle was the same as the one associated with the murder in Chicot County that would be a major break. Still, there were several similarities to the cases. However, they'd just have to wait and see how the evidence developed before they could determine the likelihood of the killer being the same person in both cases.*

The agents worked straight through lunchtime without taking a break to eat. Giordano noticed that Bouldon was beginning to get frustrated. Giordano feared there would be an explosion or, at the very least, Bouldon would become temperamental and rude. In order to redirect their efforts, he asked Whitcomb, "Can we see the body, interview the coroner and your forensics expert? Maybe they've come up with some new evidence that could be useful to our investigation."

"Sure, no problem. There could be some new developments. I haven't been updated as yet this morning. I'll give you the address of the morgue. I'm sure the Taney County Coroner and our forensic expert will be happy to talk to you about the progress of their investigation. I think they're still at the morgue gathering evidence."

"Thank you, Sergeant, we're going to eat lunch first and visit the morgue later in the afternoon." Giordano glanced at Bouldon for confirmation he was in agreement.

Bouldon nodded and Whitcomb handed him the address of the morgue. Bouldon seemed mollified and thanked Whitcomb for his help.

The agents departed the motel in their black, GMC Yukon with Anderson at the wheel. It was only a short distance to downtown Branson, where the morgue is located. They stopped briefly for a sandwich and a drink at a local root beer stand. Thirty minutes later, they parked and walked into the Taney County Morgue in the basement of the Cox Medical Center. When they arrived, they were greeted by Dr. Carl Meadows, Coroner of Taney County, and Steve Cox, the Missouri State Police forensics expert from St. Louis.

After a brief introduction, Roger Bouldon asked for an update concerning the victim, Erica Danforth. Her covered body lay on a shiny aluminum examination table in the middle of the lab. Under the sheet was the partially decomposed and autopsied corpse of Ms. Danforth. Dr. Meadows removed the sheet. "Gentlemen," he intoned gravely, "I'd like you to see the stab wounds on Ms. Danforth's chest. They are quite large. I've done a work up of the wounds and determined they probably were made by a large hunting knife." Dr. Meadows informed the agent that he and Cox, the State Police expert, who had temporarily stepped out of the room, agreed she had been stabbed to death. He went on to state that they also concluded the victim was violently raped, because of tearing in the vaginal area.

"Did you find any sperm or seminal fluid in her vagina?" Bouldon asked flatly. It was obvious that he was unaffected by the presence of the corpse.

"Strangely no, although we had expected it to be there," Dr. Meadows replied. "The assailant must have used a condom during intercourse. There is also physical evidence that the victim was alive during the rape. By the way," Dr. Meadows added, "The woman's nipples were handled very roughly. Apparently, they were abused so badly they started bleeding sometime during the attack."

Giordano took a sharp intake of breath. "That's extremely interesting!" he exclaimed interrupting the doctor. "We have a rape/murder case in Arkansas that has similarities to this case. By chance did you find any evidence of a substance that could be used as a date-rape drug? Its effects could be comparable to a very strong sedative."

"Well, there are several substances that we found in her toxicology exam that are presently being analyzed by our lab in St. Louis. We don't know what they are yet," Dr. Meadows said cautiously.

"I wouldn't be surprised if one of the substances is a date-rape drug," Giordano said. His face was aglow with hope that there would be a match with the other murder case. "Would you please send the results of your toxicology exam to our lab in Quantico, Virginia? We'd like to be able to compare your results to ours and see if it's a match to our Arkansas case."

"Sure, happy to do that, Agent Giordano. Once the exam results are available, I'll see that you get a copy immediately," Dr. Meadows promised.

* * *

After conferring with Giordano and Anderson as to whether there was anything else they should do locally, Bouldon decided he and Giordano should go to the FBI field office in St. Louis to write up their criminal case report. He knew Larcovic was anxiously waiting to read their findings.

During the drive to St. Louis, Bouldon began filling his legal pad with notes to transfer into a formal report to

Larcovic. They had a partial description of the possible assailant in the bar and a police artist's rendering of the man. The physical abuse of the victim's nipples and her torn vagina were important facts, given those similarities with their Arkansas case. If a date-rape drug was used, that would be another link. Identifying the Toyota minivan was important. It was probably used in the crime. But, if they were pursuing the same killer, that meant he had ditched the Dodge Caravan and replaced it with a Toyota Sienna.

* * *

The next day, Bouldon and Giordano were at Lambert Field in St. Louis, Missouri boarding a commercial flight back to Washington, D.C. and the BSU facility in Quantico.

Chapter 15

Bouldon and Giordano arrived at Washington National Airport at 11:00 a.m. from St. Louis, Missouri aboard a Southwestern Airlines jet. They collected their luggage, located Giordano's vehicle, and drove back to Quantico to prepare for the meeting with Larcovic. Upon their arrival at the BSU, they were informed Larcovic had unexpectedly taken the day off for personal reasons. He was scheduled to return the following day. Bouldon assumed Larcovic's day-off was to spend time with his children. Larcovic had recently been through a bitter divorce and had confided to Bouldon that he was having a hard time explaining the situation to his young kids. The ex-wife, Marcie, wasn't making matters easy for him.

Bouldon knew Larcovic had tired of his unhappy marriage and had taken a mistress. Marcie must have suspected he was having an affair, so she'd hired a private investigator to catch him in the act. Once the affair was confirmed, she confronted him and requested a divorce. Bouldon felt for his boss but was grateful for the additional time to prepare the case file for Larcovic.

Giordano was anxious to receive the toxicology report

from the Missouri State Police Laboratory to confirm whether a date/rape drug was ingested by Erica Danforth. When he sat down at his desk in the BSU office, Giordano was pleased to see the lab report on top of the stack of documents awaiting his review. The toxicology report revealed there was evidence of a date/rape drug in Ms. Danforth's system. He compared the type of drug used in Branson to the one used in the Chicot County murder case. It was a match!

Giordano tried to envision the man responsible for the two murders. He wasn't shocked that the suspect had changed his facial appearance by shaving off his goatee. Giordano guessed the suspect had not been too worried about being identified in the Foot Hills Club and Grill. Obviously, the guy didn't plan on spending much time there. The bartender stated that the suspect positioned himself sideways on the bar stool so that the video camera behind the bar would not record a clear image of his face. The bartender reported that he just got a brief look at the man's face who was sitting with Ms. Danforth. Giordano wondered whether the sketch artist's drawing of the suspect's face was accurate.

Giordano recognized the professionalism with which the unsub had sanitized the crime scene at the motel. There were no fingerprints found inside the room other than the victim's. That fact alone indicated they were not dealing with an amateur. This was an experienced killer. But why had he jimmied and broken the lock on the motel room door? Was he intentionally changing his M.O.? It was obvious that the unsub was welcomed into the room and into Ms. Danforth's queen-size bed. The presence of a sexy negligee lying next to the bed along with an empty glass that had contained red wine indicated the victim was, at first, a willing participant. The fact that Ms. Danforth had no cash or credit cards in her wallet indicated that the unsub either intended to make it look like a robbery, or maybe, theft was part of the motive. Giordano wondered whether the killer needed cash. Was he short of money after acquiring a different vehicle? The Dodge was probably traded-in to help purchase the Toyota Sienna. Still, additional cash would have been needed to make the purchase.

Giordano was not surprised that the murderer had changed vehicles. He planned to ask the BSU staff to check with auto dealerships and used car lots in Missouri and Arkansas to see if they could find a transaction in which a 1999 Dodge Caravan had been traded for a 2000, or newer, Toyota Sienna.

Giordano didn't believe Phillip Danforth had anything to do with the murder of his ex-wife. Danforth's willingness to cooperate with the investigation, passing the polygraph test, and the conviction of Danforth's innocence in the mind of an experienced local investigator, Sergeant Whitcomb, convinced Giordano. He was hopeful the investigators would recover some DNA evidence from the unsub in the motel room. If so, it could be compared to the DNA evidence found on the body of the deceased prostitute in Chicot County. If the DNA evidence matched, it would certainly confirm that both murders were done by the same man.

The description of the unsub in Branson was similar to

the man seen on the gas station video in Lake Village, Arkansas, except for the goatee and the different vehicle. Another interesting similarity to the Arkansas case was the victim's severely injured body, torn vagina, and her damaged nipples. In both cases the victims had been stabbed by a large hunting knife and were viciously ravaged. Both victims died as a result of stab wounds.

Bouldon, on the other hand, was unwilling to dismiss Phillip Danforth as a suspect; not yet, anyway. He had worked too many cases in which the evidence did not initially point to the spouse as the killer. However, the spouse was ultimately determined to be the killer in the end. However, he had to admit that much of the evidence indicated both crimes were committed by the same person. But Bouldon wanted to be sure.

Before leaving Branson, Bouldon asked Jonathon Anderson, the FBI agent from St. Louis, to interview Phillip Danforth in Springfield, Missouri. There had not been enough time for Bouldon to conduct the interview himself. Consequently, he was forced to rely on Anderson's help. Bouldon trusted Anderson with the task, because he believed Anderson was competent, respected, and a capable investigator.

Bouldon also asked Anderson to interview Sharon Westerhoff, Erica Danforth's girlfriend, who lived in Branson. She talked with Ms. Danforth just prior to Erica's departure from the Foot Hills Club and Grill the night of the murder.

Bouldon expected a detailed report from agent Anderson the following morning. He hoped the report would come sooner, but he doubted if it would. He was pleasantly surprised when he received Anderson's report later in the evening. The information about Mr. Danforth was concise and to the point. Anderson did not think Phillip Danforth had anything to do with the murder. His report echoed the same rationale Sergeant Whitcomb and the local police relied on to exonerate Mr. Danforth. Further, Anderson described credible evidence provided by Ms. Westerhoff which supported exculpation of Mr. Danforth. She claimed Mr. Danforth was still very much in love with his ex-wife. Anderson reported that she was very convincing that there was no way Mr. Danforth would have killed or paid someone to kill her friend, Erica. He was just too much in love with her and had been so hopeful of their eventual reconciliation.

The bartender at the Foot Hills Club had described the unknown person sitting at the bar with Erica Danforth as muscular with a medium-size frame. Danforth is small and certainly cannot be characterized as muscular. Westerhoff and local investigators all described Danforth as being rather wimpy. That characterization was confirmed by Anderson.

Bouldon and Giordano met in Bouldon's office late in the afternoon to compare notes and prepare for the upcoming meeting with Larcovic. Bouldon admitted that the discovery that a strong acid was used to destroy DNA evidence in the shower drain of Room 189, Erica Danforth's room, supported Giordano's contention that the two murders were connected. The two agents agreed that the unsub must have been welcomed into the room and Erica's bed. They also agreed that the damage to the lock was most likely done by the unsub after he killed Erica, but prior to his leaving the room. Bouldon agreed with Giordano that the unsub was attempting to make his M.O. appear different. Both BSU agents thought the suspect was trying to throw the authorities off his track.

The description of the suspect's hair as dark-brown was consistent. But the grey tint was inconsistent. It would be easy enough to add a grey tint by using grey hair dye, which is available in most drug stores. "Plus," Bouldon added, "if the man was there to make love to Ms. Danforth, he wouldn't have left her so quickly after sex. He would have stayed much longer." Bouldon thought for a minute and then asked, "Do you agree that – if we are dealing with the same killer – sex for this unsub is not his real purpose? It's just part of his brutal and grotesque routine."

Giordano realized Bouldon was working his way toward accepting that the two murders were related. Giordano nodded his agreement, and thought to himself that, while Bouldon could be a pain in the ass, he really respected how the senior agent tried to consider all possibilities before committing his energy to pursuing one suspect above any others.

Bouldon suggested to Giordano that they draft their individual findings separately and then get back together in the morning to formulate an official report. Giordano agreed and went back to his office to collect his thoughts. Bouldon did the same. The following morning, Bouldon and Giordano met in the conference room and drafted their report, highlighting what they agreed were the most important details.

After Larcovic arrived he immediately dove into his agents' report. The information presented convinced Larcovic to call a staff meeting to update the entire team on what Bouldon and Giordano had found. He dropped off a copy of the report to Director Underwood and circulated it to the other members of the BSU staff.

* * *

The BSU staff assembled at 2:00 p.m. Larcovic did not expect Director Underwood to attend and was surprised when, right before 2:00 p.m., Underwood walked into the conference room. He stood in front of the group and commented, "Lady and gentlemen, I think you are finally closing in on this monster. I'd like it very much if this murderer could be brought to justice in the not too distance future. Governor Huckabee, Karl Rove, President Bush's Chief of Staff, and I are relying on you to capture this murderer before he kills again. I'm thankful for your progress and I await the phone call from your Boss telling me the unsub has been captured. Proceed with your meeting," he said officiously, turned on his heel, and strode out of the room.

Larcovic stood, looked around the room and then nodded in the direction of Bouldon and then Giordano. He began, "I'm pleased to inform you that Agents Giordano and Bouldon were able to compile some pretty compelling evidence concerning our latest unsub. We have secured a police sketch of the unsub in Branson, and, so far, it appears to closely match the unsub in Chicot County. However, the eye witness in Branson only saw the suspect's face clearly for an instant, so the drawing might not be totally accurate."

He cleared his throat and continued. "Our agents, the local coroner, the Missouri State Police laboratory and their forensic experts, who performed the autopsy on the victim, have uncovered evidence linking the murder in Missouri to the one in Arkansas. We have conclusive evidence that the DNA materials found in both murder cases are from the same man. We were able to recover a small amount of cellular material from the bed sheets in the Branson case and that's how we were able to acquire the unsub's DNA evidence. Our laboratory experts compared that with the DNA found in the sperm sample on the Chicot County victim and got a positive match."

Larcovic looked around the room and noted with satisfaction that all eyes were intently on him. "The murder weapon in both cases appears to be a large hunting knife. Both victims were brutally raped and murdered. The unsub raped both victims so viciously that he torn their vaginas. Their nipples were savagely abused. The same type of date/rape drug was ingested by both victims."

Murmurs were heard around the room along with some quick scribbling on legal pads. Larcovic resumed, "Although the victim in Arkansas was much younger than the victim in Branson, both had similar traits: blond hair, small, vulnerable, and willing to have sex. We assume one for money and the other for companionship. The unsub used the same type of acid on the first victim to destroy her identity that he used to destroy DNA evidence in a shower drain in the second murder." After another pause to let that information sink in, Larcovic said, "We have reason to believe the unsub is now driving a 2000 era Toyota Sienna instead of the 1999 Dodge Caravan. As you will see from the drawing, our unsub has apparently shaved off his goatee."

With a little more enthusiasm in his tone, Larcovic went on, "We also have reason to believe the unsub is trying to change his M.O. slightly to make it look like the two murders are unrelated. But my guess is that after ten or so years of killing our unsub is not doing a very good job of changing his M.O. There are only so many things a killer can change to hide his trademark. Hopefully, he won't execute another kill for a while, as it seems he goes silent for a period of time after accomplishing one. That seems to be one of the ways he's managed to avoid capture so far. But now, we may have obtained sufficient information to identify and arrest this killer. We are going to release the drawing of the unsub to the news media and hope that someone will come forward to identify him."

Larcovic slapped the table with his palm. "If anyone on the team has doubts about my decision, speak up now." He looked around the room challenging any member of the team to disagree. When no one did, he nodded and went on in an aggressive tone. "We are going to update the profile to indicate the unsub no longer has a goatee and is driving a Toyota Sienna instead of a Dodge. I'm very hopeful we will get a tip from a civilian telling us to check out a person of interest who might end up being our unsub. It's very possible that these two cases could be wrapped up fairly quickly. We just need a little luck and some cooperation from the general public. So, let's redouble our efforts to capture this dangerous serial killer!"

Chapter 16

About ten days after the unsub's profile was updated and the police artist's drawing of the unsub appeared in most Arkansas newspapers, the Arkansas State Police received an anonymous telephone call from a middle-aged woman. The woman claimed she knew the identity of the suspect in the Chicot County murder case. She indicated she didn't want to be involved, but was willing to provide the suspect's name and address, as long as she could do so in confidence. During the call, the unidentified caller became either frightened, nervous, or changed her mind. She hung up before giving the information she claimed to possess. The BSU officials in Quantico, Virginia were immediately notified concerning the development in the case.

Unbeknownst to the caller, the State Police traced the call from Heber Springs, Arkansas to Ms. Sandy Darnell. The authorities did not know whether the call was disconnected by someone else indicating Ms. Darnell was in danger. The officer who took the call described the tone of the caller's voice as, "not sounding frightened, but definitely nervous". He turned the information over to

Sergeant Sidney Johnson, the lead investigator in charge of the Chicot County murder case. Johnson decided to go to Heber Springs and interview Ms. Darnell in person.

The following morning at 5:30 a.m. Johnson pulled his unmarked police cruiser into a parking space across the street from Sandy's Family Restaurant. He hoped the information that Ms. Darnell could provide would be useful to the investigation and it was not just the imagination of a small-town crackpot.

Johnson entered the restaurant and sat down at a booth, patiently waiting for a waitress to arrive. Within a few minutes a heavy-set, older woman came out from the kitchen with a cup of coffee and a menu. She said, "Sorry for the delay, I'm here by myself until 6:00 a.m. when the day waitress comes into work."

"No problem," Johnson said politely. "I've had a chance to check out your specials on the chalk board. Everything looks appealing, so I'm undecided. What do you recommend?"

"Well, I don't want to brag, but the locals will tell you that everything I make is delicious. Take your time and I'll be back in a couple of minutes to take your order," Sandy said smiling.

"Well, I'm leaning toward the bacon and cheese omelet, but I'll look at the menu and review the specials again," Johnson replied and returned her smile.

Sandy noted the customer was very polite and had an officious manner. He was dressed in a black suit, starched white shirt, and red tie. She knew the man was definitely not local.

When Sandy returned, Johnson said, "I'll try the bacon, Swiss-cheese omelet. No toast please," he said politely.

"Good choice," Sandy exclaimed. "It's one of my favorites."

Several minutes later, Sandy appeared with an overflowing plate of piping hot food including home fried potatoes. She slid the plate in front of him and asked, "Do you care for anything to spice it up a bit?"

"No, thank you," he said smiling. "There is enough food here to feed a small family! But it smells wonderful. I'm sure the praise locals have for your cooking is well deserved."

Sandy looked at him appreciatively and said with a broad smile, "My goal is to provide the finest tasting food in town and I don't want anyone to leave hungry. Enjoy your breakfast."

When Sandy returned to refill Johnson's coffee cup, she stated, "You're obviously not from around here. What brings you to Heber Springs?"

Johnson lowered his voice, leaned toward her, and said, "No, I'm not." He quickly pulled out his Arkansas State Police gold shield and said, "I'm Sergeant Johnson. I assume you are Sandy Darnell?"

"Yes, I am." Sandy said nervously. "What's this about?"

"You made a call yesterday afternoon to the Arkansas State Police headquarters in Little Rock claiming you could identify the Chicot County killer. However, before giving us the information you abruptly hung up the phone. Was your life in danger or was that a bad time to talk?" Johnson's expression was both sympathetic and serious.

Sandy looked around nervously and demanded, "How did you find out I was the caller?"

"Oh, we have our ways ma'am," Johnson replied mysteriously, but immediately resumed his serious tone of concern. "Are you now or were you in danger yesterday when you called?"

"No, I'm not. But I don't want my information to become public knowledge. You know, what if I'm wrong?" Sandy replied nervously.

"We won't know that until you talk to us," Johnson said gently touching Sandy's wrist empathetically. "We always appreciate cooperation, regardless of whether it turns out to be right or wrong."

"Can you come back around 9:30 after the breakfast crowd thins? I'll be in the kitchen preparing the lunch specials. We can talk then." Sandy felt a little dazed and continued to look around nervously.

"No problem, ma'am. I'll see you then," Johnson promised. "What do I owe you for breakfast?" He asked.

"With tax it will be four dollars and fifty cents."

Johnson raised his eyebrows in surprise at the modest amount charged. He left a ten-dollar bill on the table and departed the restaurant. He immediately called his boss at State Police HQ in Little Rock to report making contact with Sandy Darnell. Johnson was excited and pleased. He was convinced Darnell's evidence was going to be credible and would help them catch the killer.

* * *

At 9:30 a.m. sharp Johnson reentered the restaurant. Sandy Darnell noted Johnson had removed his suit coat and tie. He nodded at her and ambled up to the counter and took a seat looking like he was just there for brunch. Sandy casually slid a menu in front of him. A small piece of paper was clipped to the menu with the name of Michael James Trettin and a local Higden address written on the slip of paper.

The closest customer to them was out of earshot. Johnson quietly said in a reassuring tone, "Thank you, Sandy. I won't disclose your name to anyone outside of the personnel working this investigation. A policy of strict confidence will be maintained to protect your identity."

Sandy quickly looked around the restaurant. "I appreciate that very much. I don't want to get a reputation for being a snitch. I'm sorry I didn't call you back, and made you come here to see me. I didn't want to make trouble for anyone."

"I understand completely. I know what it's like in small towns," Johnson nodded sympathetically. "I have just a few questions I need to ask you about Mr. Trettin. What is his occupation?"

Sandy shot a glance down the length of the counter and then replied in a whisper, "He's in the construction business. Michael owns and operates a small handy-man service. He is very talented. He can do most jobs from start to finish. He's done work here in the restaurant."

Bingo, thought Johnson after hearing the suspect's occupation. *We've got you!* Doing his best to maintain a low even tone, Johnson asked, "Does Mr. Trettin permanently reside in Higden?"

"No, he comes to Arkansas seasonally to work. He says he likes to escape the brutal summers in Florida. He usually arrives in May and returns to Florida in the fall. But, seems like he was earlier than usual this year. Trettin told me he lives on the Gulf side of the state, but I don't know exactly where."

"Have you seen Mr. Trettin lately?" Johnson inquired calmly.

"Yes, he was here about a week ago for lunch. He was having a bad day. He seemed nervous and irritated. I asked him what was bothering him. He said something about there being a family emergency. He might be heading back to Florida earlier than he'd planned to."

"Very interesting," Johnson said nodding appreciatively. "Did he give any indication of where he was going in Florida, or ever mention a town or city?"

"Sorry, nope. Like I said, Michael never mentioned his or any address to me," Darnell shook her head sadly. "I don't know where he goes in Florida, other than he's talked about the Gulf side of the State."

"Thank you very much for your time and trouble, Ms. Darnell," Johnson said earnestly. "I may have some more questions, so please don't be surprised if I contact you again."

"Okay, just so long as it stays confidential," Sandy said as she shot another glance around the restaurant before she walked back into the kitchen.

* * *

Fifteen minutes later Johnson placed a direct call to the BSU office in Quantico, Virginia. The call was initially directed to Agent Giordano, but Johnson insisted that he had to speak directly to the agent in charge of the BSU team. Giordano reluctantly passed the call on to Gary Larcovic. After Larcovic identified himself, Johnson said, "This is Sergeant Sidney Johnson with the Arkansas State Police. Do you remember me?"

Larcovic was a bit startled, but replied in an even tone, "Yes, you are heading up the recent murder investigation in Chicot County. We met briefly. What can I do for you, Sergeant?" Larcovic asked politely.

"I think we've got the name and address of the man responsible for killing the prostitute in Chicot County."

"You do!" Larcovic's excitement rose. "Please give me the details, Sergeant."

"Yesterday, we received a call from a woman in Heber Springs, Arkansas claiming she knew the suspect we are looking for. She said his name is Michael James Trettin of Higden, Arkansas. I drove to Heber Springs to interview the woman today and she informed me Mr. Trettin works in the construction industry and temporarily resides in Arkansas but lives in Florida. She saw the unsub a week ago when he informed her that he was returning to Florida early this year to take care of a family emergency. It sounds pretty fishy to me."

"Congratulations Sergeant! It sounds like you've done some solid work. What is your next step going to be?"

"Later this evening, we plan to send a SWAT team to the suspect's home to serve a search warrant and detain him."

"If there's anything I can do to help, please let me know. I'd appreciate an updated case report too."

"Not a problem, Agent Larcovic. I've already built you into the loop. For the moment, we don't need anything, but that could change depending on circumstances. Once the suspect is in our custody, I'll interview him and let you know what we find out."

"This is great news, Sergeant Johnson. Thank you so much for your help."

"Let's just hope we can get this killer off our streets and put an end to his killing spree."

When Larcovic hung up he immediately called Director Underwood to give him an updated report on the progress of the case.

Underwood expressed his appreciation and said he

hoped this latest development would be fruitful.

"So do I," Larcovic said, then sighed and leaned back in his office chair.

* * *

In the early morning hours, a combined SWAT team from the Arkansas State Police and the Cleburne County Sheriff's Department approached the unlit home of Michael James Trettin, located just outside of Higden. The officers took up defensive positions and surrounded the property. One officer knocked on the front door and yelled, "Police!" A few seconds later a battering ram was deployed to gain entry into the home. A quick search of the property revealed that Trettin was not there. Officers found the dresser drawers in the bedroom were left open, but with clothing inside. It appeared Trettin had hastily departed the house.

In the back yard the officers discovered a 1999 Dodge Caravan covered with a tarp. They immediately began a thorough search of the property. A five-gallon white bucket with tools and a container of acid was discovered in a tool shed.

When the local authorities concluded that Michael Trettin had fled Arkansas, they notified the FBI. An all-points bulletin (APB) for Michael James Trettin, driving a 2000 Toyota Sienna, was issued. The assumption was that Trettin was in, or on his way, to Florida. Whether he was fleeing to avoid capture, or, as he had mentioned to Ms.

Sandy Darnell, there was a family emergency, was unknown.

* * *

What the authorities did not know was that Michael James Smith, aka Michael Trettin, planned to cross the United States/Mexico border to avoid capture by the police. Smith knew the border crossing from Mexico to the United States was carefully monitored, but crossing over into Mexico was much easier. Smith knew from experience that Mexican border regulations were lax, because Mexico needed tourist dollars. He figured once he got to southern Texas, he'd sell the Toyota to raise cash. Then, he'd take a bus to the border town of Laredo, Texas. From there he'd take a cab across the border and disappear undetected as just another American tourist. Michael Smith hoped that once in Mexico he could start a new life, maybe have reconstructive surgery to change his identity, and eventually resume his routine as a serial killer.

* * *

Two days earlier Smith had packed some of his essential belongings into a large suitcase and departed his home outside of Higden around 10:00 p.m. He headed west toward Oklahoma. Smith decided it would be smarter to drive on secondary roadways in Oklahoma rather than take interstates or US highways on the way to and through Texas.

Hector Sanchez was heading north from the Mexican border in a Freightliner diesel truck packed with a load of Mexican-grown tomatoes in its forty-five-foot trailer. Sanchez's first delivery in the US was scheduled at a Walmart distribution center north of Houston. Hector was cruising along the expressway listening to a CD of Mexican pop-music blaring out of the speakers inside the truck's cab.

By the time he reached Houston, Smith was sorely tired of driving state highways and secondary roads. Since he'd made it so far without incident, he decided he could risk driving US-59 the rest of the way to Laredo. He carefully kept to the speed limit of 55 miles per hour. After driving just a few minutes on US-59, to his consternation Smith noticed the presence of a Texas State Trooper in his rearview mirror. The trooper was driving fast and quickly closing on Smith's vehicle. As it approached, the cruiser's flashing lights came on and the siren sounded. The trooper came along side Smith's vehicle and signaled him to pull over.

A tremor of terror shot down Smith's spine. But he calmed himself. There was no good escape at the moment, so he decided to pull off the road and would determine what the cop wanted before he'd try anything drastic. When both cars were parked on the shoulder of the road, the officer turned on the cruiser's spotlight and directed the beam into the rear window of the Toyota. He quickly exited the squad car, removed his Glock pistol from its holster and yelled, "Driver, turn off the engine, throw the keys out on the ground, put both hands out the window, and don't you move!"

Smith rolled down the window as if he was going to comply. But as the officer approached the vehicle, he floored it and the Sienna took off spraying gravel at the trooper. There was an exit off the highway a short distance ahead. Smith sped toward the exit at full speed. The officer ran back to his car and was in pursuit with lights and siren blaring.

Smith turned onto the off ramp and then turned left onto an access road that ran parallel to the highway heading south bound. He saw in the rearview mirror that the police vehicle was in hot pursuit behind him. So, at the next opportunity Smith raced back onto the highway. The early morning traffic was heavy, and Smith hoped he could lose the police officer in the traffic separating the two vehicles.

At the next exit Smith gunned the Toyota and raced past a line of cars backed up at an interchange. Smith looked left and then right intending to turn left to go across an overpass hoping to lose the cop still stuck in traffic on the highway. Smith didn't notice the speeding Freightliner driven by Sanchez coming from his left side when he entered the intersection. His attention was diverted for the few seconds he swiveled around to look for the cop car.

BAM! The impact of the semi and the Toyota was massive. Smith's vehicle was T-boned and then propelled sideways by the powerful force of the diesel truck and heavily loaded trailer.

Smith had unbuckled his seat belt when stopped by the trooper. He didn't fasten it when he fled. Inside the Sienna after the impact by Sanchez's truck, Smith's body was thrown around the interior like he was a ball inside a pinball machine. First, he was thrown all the way across the front seats and slammed into the passenger door. Then, he was flung back and smashed into the steering wheel and then flopped against the driver-side door. For a few moments Smith was conscious of excruciating pain. His forehead was gashed open revealing skull bone. Ribs were broken on both sides. His right lung was punctured and there was massive internal bleeding from organ ruptures.

The Sienna had rolled over several times and the front of the semi was resting on top of the driver's side of the vehicle. When the semi was jacked off the Sienna, a single body was visible inside. Whether Smith uttered any last words before succumbing to the pain, no one would have heard them. By the time EMT's were able to extract him from the vehicle, Michael James Smith was dead.

* * *

After the crash scene was cleared of debris, a wrecker towed the Toyota Sienna to a warehouse where the authorities could inspect the vehicle. Inside Smith's suitcase the police found a large manila envelope with before and after photos of two dead women. One of the photographs was eventually identified as the unknown prostitute who was killed and left in the pine forest in

Chicot County. The other woman was identified as Erica J. Danforth.

The tool kit used in both crimes was left in Smith's home outside of Higden. A forensic team was able to determine that there were traces of Erica Danforth's blood on the blade of the hunting knife found with Smith's tool kit. The vise gripes had blood samples that matched the deceased prostitute.

The police laboratory in Little Rock compared the deceased driver's blood to the DNA evidence found at both crime scenes. They matched. Inside the driver's wallet, investigators found a Florida driver's license issued to a Larry Jones of Lee County, Florida and another issued to Michael James Smith, also of Lee County.

* * *

The Arkansas authorities sent the entire case file to the BSU office in Quantico, Virginia. Before the file arrived Agent Larcovic was personally informed by Sergeant Johnson about the vehicular crash and death of Michael James Smith, along with all the evidence proving the decedent was the unsub for both the Arkansas and Missouri murder cases.

Larcovic's reaction was ambivalent. He felt almost giddy that this horribly brutal serial killer was dead. But he was also disappointed that his team had failed to catch Smith.

Chapter 17

It was overcast and raining at 3:30 a.m. in Heber Springs, Arkansas while Sandy Darnell drove to work the following Monday. She wondered whether the inclimate weather would affect her business. Bad weather on Monday through Friday was always a worry, because she served dinner on those days in addition to the usual breakfast and lunch schedule. Sandy pulled her worn Chevrolet sedan into a narrow parking space, got out of the vehicle and unlocked the front door to the restaurant. She had not slept well since meeting with Sergeant Johnson of the Arkansas State Police two days ago.

Sandy wondered whether the authorities had determined if Michael Trettin was involved in the Chicot County case. Just after 5:00 a.m. the newspaper delivery boy entered the restaurant and placed two copies of the Arkansas Democratic-Gazette on the counter. Since most of the prep work for breakfast was finished, Sandy decided to take a short break and look through the newspaper. She glanced over a Houston, Texas story about a two-vehicle crash involving a death in the regional section of the newspaper. It didn't catch her interest. But when she came back to the article, her eye happened to fix on the second line, which referenced Higden. Sandy smoothed the paper out and took a seat to read carefully through the article.

Driver Dies in Car-Semi Crash

A Florida man with family ties to Higden, Arkansas was killed in a two-vehicle crash early Sunday morning. The car driven by Michael James Smith, 45, of St. James City, Florida drove into an intersection south of Houston, Texas and into the pathway of a tractor-trailer driven by Hector Sanchez, Gomez Palacio, Mexico. According to the Texas State Police, the accident occurred south of Houston near Sealy, Texas at the intersection of U.S. Highway 59 and S.R. 720 around 5:15 a.m. The 2000 Toyota Sienna driven by Smith was struck by the tractor-trailer and received heavy damage. At the time of the crash, Smith was fleeing from a Texas State trooper. Officer Donald Larson stated that he stopped Smith due to the vehicle matching the described vehicle in an FBI-issued "All Points Bulletin". However, a high-speed chase ensued when Smith disobeyed the officer's orders and fled in his vehicle. Smith was pronounced dead at 5:45 a.m. at the crash scene. His body was taken to a local hospital in Sealy, Texas for an autopsy. Sanchez did not report any injuries. The accident remains under investigation.

Sandy Darnell began to hyperventilate. She was sure that Michael James Smith was the same person as Michael

James Trettin. As the fact of his death sunk in, Sandy felt a pang of guilt. *Was she responsible for Michael's death?* Tears began to flow from her eyes. *What have I done? What if Smith - Trettin – was not the killer!* A sob wracked her body and then Sandy cried openly and loudly. She felt betrayed by Sergeant Johnson and the Arkansas State Police. *Why didn't they take Michael into custody to find out whether he was guilty or not? Instead, they chased him until he got hit by a truck and killed!* Sandy Darnell said a silent prayer for the man, Michael Trettin, who had been her friend, before heading back to the kitchen to resume her duties. She didn't want to make a spectacle of herself in front of her customers. She vowed never to contact the authorities again unless it was an emergency.

* * *

By the time Director Underwood was apprised of the details of Smith's death, Larcovic had already made arrangements for Bouldon and Giordano to return to Higden, Arkansas to help with the investigation. Larcovic, with Underwood's approval, sent another team of investigators to Michael James Smith's house located in St. James City, Lee County, Florida. He hoped that in the two houses the agents would find enough evidence to close several dozen cases he believed were likely committed by Smith over more than a decade. The plan was to thoroughly search both houses, inventory every item of property, interview neighbors and acquaintances, and compile every shred of evidence that might link Smith to a host of unsolved murders that resembled Smith's last two. Forensic evidence proved the tool kit and acid found at the Arkansas home in the initial search were used in the two most recent murders. And, since the DNA evidence from the two crime scenes matched Smith's, it seemed beyond a reasonable doubt that Smith, aka Trettin, was their man.

* * *

That afternoon, agents from the Tampa Florida FBI field office, officers from the Florida State Police, and Lee County Sheriff's department converged on the St. James City, Florida home owned by Smith. The single-story house was constructed of cement blocks, painted a bright coral color, and had a pier and a boat davit. The property was overgrown with plants, bushes, and scrubs. A small power boat covered with a plastic tarp hung from the davit over the water. The back porch of the house overlooked a wide channel connected to a small waterway directly across from Sanibel Island. The channel was lined with houseboats, trailers, and cement homes similar to Smith's. A variety of fish, birds, rodents, and tall, wild grasses inhabited the waterway.

Soon after the agents entered the Florida house they began to tear it apart in their search for evidence. They searched all the closets, the attic, garage, dressers, cabinets, and furniture. Within thirty minutes they found the fake drawer under one of the side tables in the living room overlooking the channel. Inside the drawer was a small photo album containing photographs of multiple before-and-after photos of victims. The officers were astounded Smith had left such gruesome depictions of his victims. Smith had organized the photographs by date and the state in which the murders were committed. He assigned a number to each victim.

The first set of photos was labeled "April 20, 1990 Florida #1". This presumably meant that this victim was his first kill and the murder occurred somewhere in Florida on April 20, 1990. The series of photos reflected a career of rape, torture, and murder spanning more than a decade. Smith's string of killings began in 1990 and ended in the present, July 2004.

* * *

After several hours of searching and cataloguing evidence, the FBI team in Florida called Larcovic to update him concerning the progress of their investigation. After listening to a description of the photo album and log of Smith's crimes, Larcovic couldn't help feeling amazed that Smith had been able to elude detection for so long. Smith's log indicated that the Branson killing was his thirty-seventh kill.

Larcovic wondered if Smith kept other trophies of his kills hidden in places other than the house in Florida. He knew that serial killers often keep items of jewelry, strands of victims' hair, and other mementos to help them remember their conquests. By referring back to those items, serial killers often relive their kills with perverse pleasure. The pathological enjoyment they receive by reliving a rape and murder might stave-off the desire to kill for awhile. Larcovic speculated that Smith probably used the photos for that purpose.

* * *

Back in Arkansas, Bouldon and Giordano were wrapping up that investigation. Other FBI agents were utilized in the states listed with victim photos in Smith's album. The FBI was eventually able to close twenty open cases based on the evidence found in Smith's Florida home. However, eight of the photos were of victims who could not be identified, despite that their bodies had already been found. Their cases were left open. The nine other victims recorded in Smith's log were not only unidentifiable, but no bodies were found which could be associated with the photos. Those cases were considered unsolvable and the files were placed on inactive status. Unfortunately, the identity of the young prostitute killed in the pine forest in Chicot County was never determined and her case file was placed with the inactive cases.

When it was learned that Smith had two first cousins living in the Cleburne County, Arkansas area, Giordano was assigned to find and interview them.

Billy and Harry Trettin had recently moved in together to save money. Their house was located in a secluded wooded area off the main highway leading to Heber Springs. Giordano knew they worked for a logging company and their work day ended at 5:00 p.m. He arrived at their home just before 5:00 p.m. When they pulled up in their pick-up truck half an hour later, they were surprised to be greeted by an FBI agent. Giordano opened the conversation by offering condolences to them for the death of their cousin Michael. Billy Trettin nodded in appreciation and thanked Giordano.

Giordano asked the cousins whether any arrangements for Smith's burial had been made. Billy replied, "No, but we are thinking about cremation and spreading his ashes down at Greer's Ferry Lake. We don't have any money for a proper burial and funeral," Billy said sadly.

Giordano's tone changed from sympathetic to serious. "You do know, don't you, that Michael is accused of committing thirty-seven murders during the past fourteen years? The evidence is clear, but it's too late to prosecute him, since he's deceased. Did you boys have any idea your cousin Michael was involved in any of those crimes?" Giordano didn't expect the cousins would volunteer anything helpful, but he had to run down every possibility.

Billy shook his head ruefully. "Agent Giordano, neither one of us had any idea what Michael was up to. If we'd known anything about him bein' involved with what he's accused of, we'd have tried to talk him into turnin' himself in. If he didn't, well, we'd have to. We were raised to be respectable, God-fearing people. We haven't seen much of Michael over the years since he left Higden for Florida. We don't have a lot of money but we do respect the law and love Jesus. Michael has been a troubled person for as long as we've known him, right Harry?"

Harry looked away, but nodded in agreement.

"I'm not here to make matters worse for you boys. But I have to gather all the information I can, so we can help others, who have the problems Michael had. My sole intent at this point is to try to better understand your cousin through your remembrances of his childhood and upbringing."

"Well, what would you like to know?" Harry asked.

"Did he grow up poor or was his family somewhat affluent?" Giordano inquired.

"Agent Giordano, almost everyone from this part of Arkansas grows up poor," Harry said in a serious tone. We didn't have a pot to pee in. Neither did Michael's mother, Nancy Trettin, who was basically thrown out of her house when her parents learned she was pregnant with Michael at sixteen years of age. The two of them lived in glorified shacks for a lot of years before Nancy turned to prostitution to support the family." Harry paused to scratch himself and then went on. "Of course, the family never supported it – prostitution, I mean. But they never gave her a bit of money to help out either."

"How did Michael get along with others?"

Billy answered, "He stuck to himself when he was younger, but when he got in high school he changed. He started getting' in fights and causin' trouble. We always thought it had to do with other kids talkin' bad about his mom - she bein' the town whore an' all. You can't blame

Michael for gettin' kinda prickly hearin' that kinda talk about his own mother. Over time he developed a terrible temper and it got worse until he left town."

"Did you ever see him be cruel to animals?" Giordano asked.

"Well, I guess you could say that. See, he had this runt of a dog that would shit – 'scuse my French - in their house. Nancy got sick and tired of the crap in her house, but instead of beatin' the dog, she took it out on Michael. Sometimes I'd hear him screamin' as she was beatin' him. Lucky for him though, the worst beatings she gave him was when she was overly drunk. Anyway, after he got beat for the dog shittin' in the house, Michael took that runty li'l dog outside and shot it. Left it lying in the yard until the coyotes came and drug it off. He never mentioned the name Sparky again," Harry concluded.

"Did you ever witness a time when Nancy was nice or loving to him?"

Billy spoke up, "No, I never did. But I'm sure it happened every now and again. Nancy often reminded Michael that his life depended on her and her whorin' was providing for food, clothing, and shelter for him. You could tell he never really bought that line of hers. Ya know, in a small town like Higden it can't be easy bein' the son of the town whore. To put it bluntly, Nancy was a domineering mother, heavy drinker, and a slut," Billy said earnestly.

"What did she look like?" Giordano asked innocently.

"When she was sober, she cleaned up real nice. She

was short, petite, and had a real nice figure. She almost always wore tight jeans, high heels, had long blond hair and gorgeous blue eyes."

"Where is she now?"

"She was murdered in April 1980," Harry said shaking his head sadly. "The cops always thought it was one of her regular Johns that did it. But nobody could ever prove it. So, her murder is still unsolved to this very day. Michael had already left for Florida several years before she was killed."

"What about Michael's father?

"He never knew who is father was," Billy replied. "Seems mighty peculiar, but Nancy claimed she knew, but never would tell Michael or Emily Ann who their fathers were."

"Who is Emily Ann?" Giordano asked his curiosity apparently piqued.

"Oh, you didn't know Michael had a younger sister?" Billy responded with surprise. "Sorry, I just figured you already knew about her."

"No, I didn't know he had a sister. How old is she?" Giordano asked with increasing interest.

"Well, le'me think for a minute," Billy pondered the question and then said, "She oughta be about forty-one years old by now."

"Yup!" Harry interjected. "Michael turned forty-five this year, and he's four or five years older than she is."

"What do you know about her?" Giordano asked seriously.

"Not really that much," Billy said thoughtfully. "After Nancy got arrested for prostitution the Court took Emily Ann away from the family and placed her in a foster home. Her foster parents ended up adopting her sometime later. Not sure where she is now. Harry and I kinda lost touch with the girl. After her adoption, the family moved to Tennessee and that's the last time we saw her. One time, we heard she was killed in a home fire but we never got anything official about it. As far as we know, she might be dead. And, that's exactly what I told Michael this year at Homecoming."

Chapter 18

On a hot and sultry afternoon in Nettleton, Mississippi an attractive 41-year-old blond sat in her rocking chair in a pair of tight jeans, a colorful blouse, and sandals gazing at the traffic a mile from her covered porch. A reliable Chevrolet sedan was parked in the driveway of her modest home. The lawn was well tended and a beautiful flower and vegetable garden were laid out in a side yard.

All seemed well in Ann Haskins little world in rural northern Mississippi. She was gainfully employed in Tupelo. Her home was fifteen miles to the southwest on the main highway leading into Nettleton, Mississippi. Gazing off into the countryside Ann could see a hilly terrain. To the west, she could see outlines of fields of soybeans, cotton, and rice, crops which were common in northern Mississippi.

It was a muggy day and the temperature soared into the mid-eighties. Ann poured herself a glass of cold, sweet tea from a pitcher she had prepared that morning. She was waiting for Teresa Jones, her co-worker, to arrive. An occasional gust of wind gave Ann a brief respite from the heat.

When she was officially adopted, Emily Ann Trettin's name was changed to Ann Haskins.

About fifteen minutes after she began sipping her sweet tea Ann saw a familiar vehicle driving down her lane. The vehicle stopped in front of her home and a petite, young African-American woman got out of the car carrying a bag full of clothing. Teresa Jones quickly climbed the steps to the porch and greeted Ann brightly. "Afternoon missy, sure, is a hot one today."

"It sure is, Teresa." Ann returned her friend's smile. "Can I offer you a glass of cold tea for your trouble?"

"Thank you, but not this time. My boyfriend is waiting to take me to lunch. Another time, okay Ann?"

"That'll be fine. Don't forget to tell Mrs. Peters I'll have the clothes ready by tomorrow afternoon. And remind her that I'd appreciate cash for doing the alterations so quickly."

"I surely will, honey. Mrs. Peters knows how fortunate she is to have such a capable and dependable seamstress as you."

"I'm sure it won't be a problem, but I like to remind her every now and then. She knows I like cash. Besides, we've been so busy this week, I'm sure cash won't be a problem," Ann said with a wink. "You know, I can always use the extra money."

"You said it, honey. Me too!" Jones said with a chuckle. "I've been saving to go see my older sister's family in Mobile, Alabama and every little bit helps."

John W. Gemmer

"Well that sounds really nice, Teresa. We all deserve a nice little vacation now and then," Ann said with an intimate smile. "Thank you for bringing the clothes out to me. It saved me a trip and I sure appreciate it," Ann said sincerely.

"No problem, honey. You know I just love seein' your flower garden. It's so pretty! And the aromas and fragrances from those flowers are so unique. It's to die for!"

"Thank you so much," Ann replied. "I have over twenty varieties of flowers in the garden and each type of flower has its own special fragrance. I think it makes for a delightful blend."

"I sure agree with that. But I gotta go now," Jones said and then turned and hurried down the porch steps. "I don't want to be late for my date. See you tomorrow, Ann."

Ann waved and called to her friend as Jones got into her car, "Tell Maureen I'll be there after lunch!"

Ann sat a little while longer after Jones left enjoying her sweet tea and the view from her porch. Then she picked up the bag of clothes, glass, and pitcher of tea and went inside to her sewing room to begin her work.

* * *

Ann lived alone. She was generally content with her life, but occasionally her isolation out in the country got to be too boring. She had no regular social life, and, despite

203

being an attractive unmarried woman, she did not have a boyfriend or any romantic interest. When her physical need for sex motivated her, she would go out of town and procure a man to take care of her needs. But other than the occasional erotic adventure, the quiet peacefulness and serenity of life in Nettleton appealed to her.

While Ann worked on the alteration of a petite, stylish, and colorful dress, it reminded her of pleasant times back in Higden, Arkansas when she was a young girl learning to sew at the foot of her grandmother. Almost every day after school she would go to her grandparents' house for a few hours before heading home. Ann hated going home to her mother, but looked forward to seeing her older brother Michael. Compared to their erratic and sometimes violent mother, Michael was a stabilizing influence in Ann's life and she loved him. Many times, during their childhood Michael stood up to their mother and convinced her to beat him instead of her. When their mother was angry, which occurred mostly when she was drunk, she turned violent and wanted to take it out on her children. While Ann had never been beaten by her mother the way Michael was, she was frequently emotionally abused. For years Ann pondered whether it would have been worse to be physically abused. Ann finally decided emotional abuse was even worse.

On occasion, after Ann reached puberty, some of her mother's so-called suitors, who were usually drunk, would go into Emily Ann's bedroom and try to molest her. If Michael was home, he would scream, yell, and threaten until the man left her alone. Ann had awful memories of being physically abused on more than one occasion by middle-aged men preying on her as a young girl. She didn't know for sure whether her mother encouraged the activity, but she suspected she might have. Whenever she thought about that, she shook her head and tried to drive away the disgusting images of her mostly-miserable upbringing.

She did, however, have pleasant memories of being at home with Michael when he taught her to fix simple mechanical things on their family pick-up truck. Emily Ann was mechanically inclined and she enjoyed working on the truck. Michael showed her how to handle some of the routine maintenance items, like oil change, timing, tires, and brakes. Michael let her help him perform some rudimentary home construction projects too, like wiring boxes and switches, doing framing and drywall repair, and painting. Emily Ann was interested and a quick student for those tasks as well. Nancy completely relied on her children to keep the home in good working order. She proclaimed that those projects were part of their responsibility to the family, just like her job was to provide for their food, clothing, and housing by prostituting herself.

In 1976 Nancy Trettin was arrested for theft by the Cleburne County Sheriff's Department. Child Protective Services was ordered by the Cleburne County Superior Court to place Emily Ann Trettin in a foster home until her mother finished her year-long sentence. Ann was treated well by the foster family. When she was required to move back home with her mother, it did not go well. The emotional abuse started right up again and continued until her mother was arrested for prostitution a year later. Emily

Ann was placed into another foster home. These foster parents seemed loving and concerned about her well-being. So much so that they petitioned the Court to adopt Emily Ann. The Court eventually terminated Nancy's parental rights and granted the adoption petition.

Michael lived in several foster homes. His delinquency from school, defiant attitude, and unruly behavior resulted in multiple placements. Nancy didn't contest Michael's foster placements. She even testified in court that he was uncontrollable. So, Michael and Emily Ann were separated by placement in different foster homes.

Emily Ann eventually learned that Michael had left Higden to live in Florida. The separation made Emily Ann feel terrible, but there wasn't anything she could do about it.

As her thoughts returned to her sewing, the continuous pounding noise of the machine in its repetitious and rhythmic work awakened a vivid memory. Ann recalled how her adoptive father, Elliot Haskins, who by then she called Dad, molested her. She remembered lying face down in bed, half-asleep, and feeling a hand probing around her privates under the covers. At first, she thought she was dreaming, but soon realized it was no dream. She could smell her father's garlic breath. She quickly turned to avoid his sexual advances. She recalled yelling, "What the fuck are you doing to me?" She squirmed away from him, jumped out of bed, and ran into the kitchen where her mother, Beverly Haskins, was cooking. "Do you know what your husband just did to me?" She screamed.

"I think I do," her Mother replied calmly. "He told me

he was going in to wake you up for dinner."

"Yes, he did that, but he also fondled my privates," Ann said through tears.

"Ann, how dare you talk about your loving father that way," Beverly said in a disappointed tone. She seemed determined to act as if nothing happened. "Maybe you were sleeping and just imagined it. Don't you think that's a possibility?"

"No, I think I know the difference." Ann was disgusted with her dad and losing patience with her mom. *Why did she not believe me?*

Beverly insisted that Ann had been asleep and had misunderstood Elliot's touching her on the buttocks to wake her up.

Over time, Elliot's predatory behavior continued and his attempts to molest Ann became more aggressive. Beverly refused to believe anything inappropriate was happening.

Eventually Ann realized that Beverly Haskins was intentionally ignoring the reality of her husband's inappropriate sexual advances. Elliot Haskins was a sexual predator preying on their adopted daughter and Beverly knew it, but she didn't want to admit it to herself.

After the Haskins family moved to Nashville, Tennessee in late 1980 for a more lucrative position for Elliot, Ann gave in to him. She was seventeen. She hated it each time he touched her, and she hated herself for letting him do it. She wanted to get out and get away from the sexual abuse, but she realized that she had no way of supporting herself without the Haskins. Nancy Trettin was murdered in early 1980, but left no estate or life insurance for her children. She had debts and by the time the house was sold and the bills were all paid, there was nothing left.

In 1982 there was a terrible fire at the Haskin's home. Ann was lucky to survive almost unscathed when fire fighters rescued her in the bathroom. They found her lying naked in the bath tub submerged under water for her protection. Elliot and Beverly both perished in the fire. The cause and origin of the deadly fire puzzled the local fire marshal. But there was no formal finding of arson.

Ann was the sole survivor and beneficiary of the Haskins' estate. Elliot's engineering firm had taken out a million-dollar term-life insurance policy on him as part of his employee-benefits package. Elliot's death was ruled to be an accident. Because the policy contained a double indemnity clause, Ann received two million-dollars.

After the insurance policy paid off and her parents' estate was closed by the probate court, Ann had more than enough money to leave Nashville and move to her choice of a new town to start a new life. Eventually, she chose Nettleton, Mississippi. She paid cash for her modest home in the countryside, bought a reliable automobile, and established an adequate nest egg managed by a local bank's trust department. She worked as a seamstress, which paid well enough to cover basic living expenses. She seemed to be living a respectable, yet isolated, existence. Ann generally felt good about herself and how her life was going.

While she waited for the insurance company and the

fire marshal to determine the cause of her parents' deaths, and the probate court to settle the estate, Ann had no income or access to funds. So, while she waited to receive her inheritance, Ann tried to support herself by strip dancing at a high-end gentlemen's club in downtown Nashville called The Velvet Kitten. The club specialized in young, vibrant, pretty women. Ann experimented with prostitution to supplement tips from erotic dancing. Why not? Wasn't that how her real mother made a living? But it made her feel degraded, used, and taken advantage of. After a few months, Ann stopped having sex for money, quit stripping, and holed up in a cheap motel waiting for the estate to settle. She tried to heal the emotional abuse to her psyche.

While awaiting the estate to settle, Ann began thinking about moving somewhere unknown to her, a place she could start a new life far away from Higden and Nashville. She fantasized about being anonymous and free to live a completely different and meaningful life, separated from the abuses of her past. Ann wondered whether she would ever be able to establish a significant and loving relationship with either a man or a woman. She had tried both, but soon discovered she was more interested in the affection of a man. But, trusting someone - hell trusting anyone - would be a challenge for her. She thought that, if she took her time, she might meet someone who would be willing to take care of her and be understanding of her past. Ann thought she might be so broken she would never be able to have a normal life. Nancy and her unscrupulous suitors, Elliot Haskins, and her own attempt at prostitution, turned Ann into a broken, lost soul.

During that period in her life, Ann often thought about a Bible verse from the New Testament that her grandmother taught her. It was Romans 3:23-25: "For all have sinned and fall short of the glory of God, and are justified by his grace as a gift, through the redemption that is in Christ Jesus, whom God put forward as a propitiation by his blood, to be received by faith." She thought she understood the meaning and wondered, but doubted, whether it could apply to her.

In the summer of 1984 on a short vacation trip through the Deep South, Ann decided to stop in Memphis, Tennessee to visit Graceland and see Elvis Presley's grave. She had planned to check out Birmingham, Alabama next, but drove into Nettleton on the way to Tupelo, Mississippi. She stopped at a local church for Sunday services. The church was non-denominational and was called The Redemption Place. Something about the church, the parishioners, and the pastor impressed her. It spoke to her soul. That's all it took. She decided to move to Nettleton, Mississippi and put down roots. And that's where she's lived for twenty years.

Ann purchased the 1,200 square-foot house outside of town. Nettleton seemed like the paradise she had dreamed of her entire life. Ann liked to garden and so she planted many varieties of flowers and vegetables in her side yard. Although the impulse surprised her, Ann decided to honor her natural mother's death by planting several red rose bushes in her garden to commemorate Nancy's passing.

Emily Ann Trettin thought that someday she might be able to forgive her mother for all the emotional abuse she had suffered directly, and indirectly, on account of her mother. And, Emily Ann wanted to forgive herself for whatever responsibility she bore for the fiascos in her life. However, she understood it was going to be easier said than done. There were things that had occurred in Ann's life that couldn't be forgiven. She had been raised by her grandmother to be aware of her sinfulness and she was certainly aware of her sinful actions. Ann blamed her mother for many of those things, but she also recognized that she had to take responsibility for decisions she made and actions she took. She wondered whether redemption would ever be possible for her.

* * *

Ann continued working on the alterations until just before sunset, when she finally stopped sewing. She let her dog, Willy, outside to do his business. Next, she went to the kitchen and prepared a chicken breast and a salad for her supper. There wasn't anything exciting to watch on television, so she picked up her Bible and began to read scriptures. Pastor Bob Sayers encouraged all his parishioners to study several Bible passages during the week related to the topic of his sermon that upcoming Sunday.

On the first Sunday of every month the congregation had a pot luck lunch after church. Ann always brought a dish to share. Ann realized the potluck lunches were a good way to get to know her neighbors and make new friends. But Ann was very shy and reserved, so she made few friends in the church even though she had become a member of the congregation.

The monthly lunches sort of reminded her of Homecoming back in Higden, Arkansas. It was always a fun event, full of children and adults, mostly conversing and getting to know their fellow parishioners. There was always way too much food. Ann regretted not returning to Higden for Homecoming, but she was still ashamed of her mother's reprehensible behavior and bad reputation.

* * *

At 9:00 p.m. Ann locked both doors, turned on the fan in the bedroom, and climbed into bed. Willy, her rescue dog, a young pit bull, jumped on top of the comforter and cuddled up next to her. Ann shut off the light and went to sleep. An hour later she awoke from a bad dream. To shake off the distress of the nightmare she made a mental list of the activities she planned for the following day.

Emily Ann Trettin, aka Ann Haskins, had no idea that the activities she planned for the following day would be interrupted by surprise visits of local police and an FBI agent.

Chapter 19

On Tuesday at 9:30 a.m. Bouldon and Giordano were wrapping up the investigation at Michael Trettin's house in rural Higden, Arkansas. Bouldon called Larcovic to check-in on the overall progress of the investigation. Larcovic informed him that they had located Emily Ann Trettin. Her name was changed in 1981 to Ann Haskins when she was adopted by Elliot and Beverly Haskins. She currently lived in rural Nettleton, Mississippi and was gainfully employed as a seamstress in Maureen Peters's Dress Shop in Tupelo. The local police were scheduled to visit Ann and inform her of the death of her brother that morning.

Giordano imagined that Ann would probably be surprised to learn about her brother Michael's death, since they had not been in contact for many years. She would undoubtedly be shocked to learn that he was a serial killer. Giordano felt a sense of relief that the local guys had the unpleasant task of making the initial contact to break the news to her. The job of extensively interviewing Ann Haskins was going to be unpleasant enough, but Larcovic and Bouldon had been very specific about his task. They wanted to know everything she knew about her brother's life in Higden. As the junior agent on the team he was not given a choice in the matter.

Giordano sighed as he climbed into the black Chevrolet police cruiser he was assigned for the drive to Nettleton, Mississippi. He estimated it would be about a five-hour drive, which he was not looking forward to. But, at least he would have more than enough time to collect his thoughts and plan his approach to, and interview of, Michael Trettin's sister. The death of a family member, no matter the circumstances, always complicated an interview. Giordano knew that deep-rooted feelings, whether they were positive or negative, could influence the outcome of the interview.

* * *

Just before 4:00 p.m. Giordano pulled into the narrow lane at 50055 U.S. Highway 45 just outside Nettleton. In the distance, Giordano could see a small, single-story home. There was a white sedan parked in the drive. Next to the driveway was a large garden filled with a variety of flowers and plants. He pulled up next to the sidewalk and got out of the vehicle, went to the door, and knocked on the screen door. An annoying smell, somewhat reminiscent of decaying flesh, mixed with the smell of fragrant flowers assaulted his olfactory sense. He could hear the sound of faint crying coming from inside the house. He peered through the screen on the door and could see a petite woman sitting on a couch reading something. He knocked again. The woman looked up, dried her eyes, collected herself, and came to the door.

Giordano cleared his throat and asked, "May I speak to Ann Haskins, please? I'm agent Frank Giordano from the FBI."

Ann Haskins blinked hard and then lifted her head and said, "I'm Ann. What can I do for you?"

Giordano was surprised by how attractive the petite, albeit middle-aged woman was. He gulped self-consciously. Ann Haskins wasn't a knockout, but she was very pretty in a "girl-next-door" way. The picture he'd conjured up of the sister of the serial killer they'd been tracking was of a more ordinary-looking woman. He imagined her to be slightly overweight, possibly unhealthy looking, and unpolished. He reminded himself that he was married and exercised all the discipline of his training not to be overcome by her sparkling blue eyes, Marilyn Monroe blond hair and figure. He nervously twisted his wedding ring with his right thumb and forefinger but then said in a carefully professional tone, "Uh, yes. I've come to see you concerning the events surrounding your brother Michael's recent death."

Ann glanced at Giordano's wedding ring and then shot back, "Isn't it a little late for that, don't you think?" She sniffled., then went on, "It's been a terrible day for me, as I hope you can imagine."

"Yes, I'm sure it has been," Giordano replied earnestly. "But I've come a long way to talk with you. However, if you prefer, I can get a room and come back in the morning?"

"If you don't mind, that would probably be better," Ann said with downcast eyes.

Giordano was disappointed, but quickly agreed. "How about I come back for a few hours tomorrow morning?"

"Yes, that would be better. I'm sure I'll feel more up to answering your questions after I've had more time to process my brother's death."

But Giordano couldn't help himself. He wanted to press on with the investigation and not waste valuable time. So, he smiled engagingly and asked, "Is that wonderful smell a pot roast by chance? Being on the road constantly I miss having a home-cooked meal."

"Oh, you haven't had supper yet, Agent Giordano?" Ann seemed to brighten a little.

"No, I've been driving all day to get here to talk to you. I've had nothing to eat, except a cheeseburger and a Coke."

"Well, neither have I," Ann said finally looking directly into Giordano's eyes. "It might be good to have company tonight. Do you like meatloaf?"

"As a matter of fact, I do. Thank you for the generous offer, but I shouldn't trouble you." Giordano said deprecatingly while hoping she would press him to stay.

"It's no trouble. I've already put it in the oven. It will be ready in less than half an hour. We can talk before and after dinner," Ann said decisively as she opened the door to let Agent Giordano enter her house.

"I guess it will be alright," Giordano said as he stepped inside. He knew it was inappropriate to accept a meal from an interviewee. It was one thing to buy an informant a meal and another to accept any kind of gratuity from someone being interviewed as part of a criminal investigation. But she wasn't a suspect or wanted for any crime. She wasn't even a witness to any crime. Her information was just needed for background. So, he decided to accept her offer.

After they were seated in the living room, as an icebreaker Giordano asked, "Ms. Haskins, how long have you been gardening?"

"Oh, I guess most of my life. The garden was much smaller when I moved here in 1984." Ann shook her head and smiled just a little. "But as you can see, it has kind of taken over most of my side yard. It just seems to get a little bigger each year." Her smile widened. "It keeps me busy and I enjoy it."

Giordano leapt at the opening she'd given him by referencing "most of my life". He wanted to press her about her childhood in Higden. But he just casually asked, "Did you have a garden growing up?"

"Well, I kind of did. It was my grandfather's, but he let me help him plant the vegetables, fertilize the plants, pick weeds, and harvest the crops."

"Was Michael involved with the garden too?" Giordano asked, but suppressing his excitement.

"No, he was never interested in that kind of thing."

The door was opened, so Giordano decided to take the

risk and press on. "Ms. Haskins, what kind of things was Michael interested in doing when you were kids?"

"From an early age Michael had an aptitude for auto mechanics and home construction. He was good at both," Ann said looking off into the distance. She returned her gaze to Giordano and shrugged. "He taught me how to make simple repairs on cars and around the house. Nothing terribly complicated, but he was a good teacher," she said wistfully.

"Did Michael enjoy school? Did he have lots of friends?"

"I don't think Michael enjoyed school and he had very few friends. Our mother always saw to that. She kept us both busy working around the house and taking care of things."

"What kinds of things are you referring to?"

"You know, maintenance projects around the house; really anything that needed to be done that she didn't want to do." There was just a touch of spite in Ann's tone.

"What did your mother do for a living?" Giordano asked, although he knew what Nancy Trettin did for a living.

"She was a prostitute, an alcoholic, and a criminal." Ann said plainly and unapologetically.

Giordano raised his eyebrows in mock surprise. He appreciated her frank honesty. But despite her direct responses to his questions, he could tell she was a little tired and still distraught from the news about her brother.

Giordano looked at his watch and said, "It's been almost twenty minutes. Is it time to take a break?"

Ann looked at him gratefully. "Yes, let's do. The meatloaf smells done." She led him to the kitchen table, gestured at a chair, and simply said, "Let's eat."

* * *

After dinner, Giordano patiently bided his time before resuming his questions. He offered to help with the dishes. Ann declined his offer. Giordano wandered around the dining room and then back into the living room looking at nick-knacks and art decorating the walls. He hoped Ann would feel more relaxed after she cleaned up the kitchen, but he desperately wanted to resume the interview.

When they were seated in the living room again, Giordano thanked her for the delicious meal and her warm hospitality. But then he turned serious. "Ms. Haskins, I know you're aware that Michael was involved in many gruesome crimes. Did it surprise you, when you were informed that your brother is a presumed serial murderer?"

She looked directly into his eyes, but replied evenly. "I was totally shocked. Maybe I was too close to the situation to imagine he could do anything like what he's accused of. I mean, who would ever think their own brother could be a serial killer?" She paused and looked around, but then went on. "But, if I were to give you an educated guess, I suppose I would say he was taking out his anger with our mother on those other women."

"Did he ever exhibit violent behavior?"

"He'd get into fights at school with his classmates, but you know how boys can be, Agent Giordano."

"Would you say he was a reclusive person, or not?"

"No, I'd say he was busy helping out around the house, working for our grandparents and taking care of Sparky, his dog."

Ann looked away, and Giordano wondered whether she knew Michael shot his own pet. He decided to press her. "Why did your brother shoot Sparky, Ms. Haskins?"

"How do you know about that?" Ann's tone became defensive for the first time.

"I met with your two cousins in Higden the other day. They told me about the incident," Giordano replied frankly.

"I see," Ann said while studying her fingers. When she looked up her tone was once again open and honest. "Our mother didn't like it when Sparky went to the bathroom inside the house. One time she stepped in the dog's poop and became extremely angry. She gave Michael a choice. She told him either she was going to kill the dog or he was. Michael took care of it but he never forgave her for it. He loved Sparky. That dog was his best friend."

"Would you consider Michael to have been book smart? For example, did he get good grades?"

"Once, I overheard our mother talking to a school official who came to the house to talk to her about Michael skipping school. From what I gathered, the truant officer told her that Michael had a high potential for learning and a relatively high IQ. So yeah, he was pretty smart," A proud smile stole across Ann's pretty face. "But that's different from being a good student – which he wasn't."

"How did you and Michael get along with your mother? Was the relationship friendly, loving, or cordial? Or, how would you describe it?" Giordano moved to the edge of his seat with anticipation, but maintained a mask of patience as if they were just making conversation. After talking to the cousins, Giordano was keen to hear what Ann had to say about the mother-son relationship.

"I'd describe it more of an accommodation than a relationship. Our mother didn't give two shits about either one of us." Ann laughed derisively. "She told us that in so many words over the years. We tried to love her; after all, she was our mother. But she placed so many impediments on us, eventually I think we both thought of her more like a keeper than a mother. Even when we were little, she tried to get rid of us more than a few times. That's when our grandpa and grandma stepped in and said they would try to help out – which they did for a few years. But when she decided to become a prostitute everything changed for the worse." Ann brushed her bangs aside and looked away.

Giordano looked at his watch. It was half past eight. He gave Ann a sympathetic look. "It's been a long day for the both of us. Let's call it quits for the evening and resume tomorrow morning. How does that sound?"

"How much longer do you think the interview will take?" Ann asked pointedly.

"I'll check my notes and let you know in the morning, but I think we can wrap this up and I can be on my way by eleven tomorrow morning," Giordano said eagerly.

"Well, I have to be in Tupelo tomorrow by noon," Ann said seriously.

"I can make that work. Can we get started by no later than 9:30 a.m.?"

Ann rose from the couch, extended her hand, and said, "See you in the morning, Agent Giordano."

They walked to the front door. Ann turned the outside light on for him. When she opened the door, with his keen sense of smell Giordano once again noticed the annoying odor. He supposed that out in the countryside there were lots of odors he, being a creature of the city, was not used to. Still, it left an impression in his memory bank.

"See you in the morning, Ms. Haskins."

Giordano waved as he started the car and maneuvered out of the driveway. Driving along Highway 45, Giordano contemplated several remaining items he wanted to ask Ann before concluding the interview.

About fifteen minutes later, he located a Holiday Inn and got a room for the night. Giordano opened his briefcase and spread several cases files on top of the bedspread. There were several things he wanted to look at one more time. At 11:00 p.m. Giordano turned off the table lamp and went to sleep.

Chapter 20

At 5:30 a.m. Ann Haskins awoke unexpectedly. Her sleep was troubled for most of the night. The visit by Agent Giordano was unsettling. She wondered whether he was after more than what he'd told her that evening. *What was he really doing here?* She hoped the reason for his questions was just to find out about Michael rather than her. Ann could hardly wait for Giordano to leave and be out of her life; forever she hoped. *Perhaps I can charm him sufficiently that he'll leave, and I'll be no more than the pleasant memory of a married man.*

* * *

Giordano was up early and finished breakfast by 8:00 a.m. He was ready to go back to Ann Haskin's house before 9:00 a.m. Traffic moved quickly along highway 45 and by 9:20 a.m. he pulled into Ann's lane. She appeared on the porch as he pulled into the driveway at her house.

Ann was fashionably dressed. She wore a colorful blue and white pinstriped dress with sandals. She had applied just the right amount of makeup and lip stick to enhance her already pretty face. Her deep blue eyes sparkled in the sunshine as did her blond hair. Once again, Giordano was stunned by how attractive she looked. "Good morning, Ms. Haskins," Giordano said politely. "How did you sleep last night?"

"Just like a baby," Ann said lying through her teeth. "Have you had breakfast yet?"

"Yes, first thing this morning," Giordano said regretfully thinking she was about to offer to make him breakfast.

"Well, I thought we could go to my favorite place for breakfast and talk there."

"Oh! Well sure, that would be fine," Giordano said trying to hide his disappointment at not being invited in for more of Ann's tasty cooking.

"I guess we still can. That is, if you don't mind watching me eat," she said with a grin. "If you follow me it's only a few miles down the road. They have wonderful sweet rolls," she said enticingly.

"That sounds great," he said returning her smile. "I'll follow you."

Several minutes later, Giordano followed Ann into the parking lot of Shirley's Restaurant. They got out of their vehicles and sat down in a booth near the front door. A waitress brought them coffee and Ann ordered a sweet roll.

Giordano decided to jump right back into interview mode by asking, "What happened to your mother?"

"She was killed on April 11, 1980 in Higden, Arkansas. The police found her body at home in the kitchen, lying on the floor. The autopsy revealed that she had been stabbed to death."

"I looked at the file, and surprisingly the exact date of her murder was not clear." Giordano gave her a quizzical look. "Why did you specify that particular date as the date of your mother's death?"

"Really? I always thought that was the day she passed based on what the police told me." Ann's friendly demeanor changed. She looked around nervously. "Of course, I could be wrong. Why do you ask, Agent Giordano?"

"I just thought it odd that you had the date engraved on her tombstone without knowing the actual date."

"Well, the funeral director in Higden asked me for her birth and death dates and so I gave him what I thought was the right date. He told me that we had to put a date of death on the tombstone," she added defensively.

"Oh, I see. It's nothing to worry about. I was just trying to clean up some questions that have arisen during the investigation."

"Okay. So, do you have any other questions about my mother's death?" Ann's calm appearance returned.

"Well, do you think your brother was capable of murdering her?"

Ann looked relieved at the question, which seemed odd to Giordano. She answered, "After finding out about the horrible crimes he committed I suppose anything is possible." Ann gave Giordano a meaningful look. "But still, I doubt it because he was living in Florida at the time."

"How do you know that, Ms. Haskins?" Giordano asked bluntly.

"Well, I guess I don't for sure but you'll undoubtedly figure it out," Ann said coldly and looked away.

"Has Michael been in touch with you at all during the last fifteen or sixteen years?"

"No, remember I told you last night that I never saw him after he left for Florida," Ann replied firmly.

"Do you know whether he has talked to anyone in Higden since he left for Florida?"

"I have no idea. Unfortunately – or maybe fortunately – after he left Higden I never heard from him and I didn't try to find him."

"I appreciate your cooperation, Ms. Haskins, and I have just one final question. And then I think we'll probably be done." He looked directly into her eyes. "Did you ever encourage or request Michael to kill your mother for revenge?"

"Agent Giordano! I would never do such a terrible thing!" Ann appeared visibly upset. She gulped and said, "After all, she was my mother. You should be ashamed of yourself to ask such a question." Ann let out a little whimper. "That's enough questions. I need to be leaving for work in Tupelo." She waved at the waitress to bring the bill. "I hope you appreciate how cooperative I've been, and" she said defiantly, "I hope our paths never cross again!"

Giordano looked unperturbed, but replied, "I apologize, Ms. Haskins. If you consider my methods unnecessarily rude or inappropriate, please forgive me. Sometimes I am overzealous in the way I approach my job. Despite the unfortunate circumstances, it was nice meeting you. You seem like a fine person, and I want to again express my condolences for your loss."

Ann sniffled, and then said, "Sorry I got upset, Agent Giordano." She sighed and appeared to have cooled down. "Maybe I'm just over reacting because of the stress of losing Michael and finding out about his terrible past." Ann was relieved that Giordano was concluding the investigation as it related to her. But she noted disconcertingly that he had left open the possibility of further questioning. That frightened her.

Several minutes later the bill arrived. Agent Giordano insisted that he would pay for her coffee and sweet roll. When they exited the restaurant, he extended his hand and thanked her again for her cooperation. Giordano watched thoughtfully as Ms. Haskins drove off. While driving back on Highway 45, Giordano had a nagging suspicion that he had not uncovered everything in the interview. Despite her apparent willingness to cooperate, and her charming attractiveness, something in his gut told him that Ann knew more than she admitted.

When he called in to report to Larcovic, and when he talked with Bouldon over coffee, Giordano expressed his suspicion as best he could. He told his superiors that he wanted to study the case files again, particularly the file they'd acquired on Nancy Trettin. Maybe there was something in there that would click, given what he'd learned, and hadn't learned, from Ann Haskins.

The next day he and Bouldon boarded a Delta Flight from Little Rock to Washington. They arrived in Quantico early in the afternoon.

Chapter 21

Giordano began to pore over the case files. There was no doubt as to the guilt of Michael James Smith. He was responsible for killing at least thirty-seven victims. But what about his sister, Ann Haskins? Why did he have this nagging feeling that she was not totally innocent? Was she really just a bystander to the carnage her brother left in his wake? Giordano was determined to answer those questions before he would close the case and put it to rest.

As to Nancy Trettin's murder, according to the police file, she was killed with a butcher knife in her own kitchen. The body wasn't found for more than a week. The coroner had pegged the time of death as being a week or more prior to finding the body. The most likely time frame was July 10th to the 14th. Ann Haskins told the mortician to use July 11, 1980 as the date on the tombstone. Why did she pick that specific date, when the coroner had only specified a range, not that particular date? Giordano found Ann's explanation rather suspicious as to why the date of death on the tombstone was July 11. But he knew that wasn't enough to consider her a suspect. Besides, the investigators verified that she was on a date that evening with her boyfriend. Her alibi seemed rock-solid.

However, when Giordano discovered that her boyfriend ended up dead in an automobile accident a few weeks later, he decided it might be worthwhile to look further into the case. He learned that the Cleburne County police handled the investigation. The cause of the accident was determined to be a faulty brake system. Her boyfriend had collided with a tree after running off the road at a high rate of speed. Emily Ann Trettin's boyfriend died instantly of a skull fracture.

During his interview with Ms. Haskins she commented that Michael had taught her how to do maintenance projects around the house, as well as basic auto mechanics. Giordano wondered whether she learned how to replace brakes on an automobile. He had to admit that Ann's good looks and pleasant character might have influenced him to be less assertive than professionally required in an interview. Yes, he admitted to himself that he was attracted to her, but still, his investigator's instinct later kicked in and raised his suspicions. Was it possible that Ann Haskins was a conniving and ruthless killer too? Surely not! It would be extremely unusual for siblings, particularly a sister, to be murderers in unrelated cases. Yet, he wasn't ready to let go of his suspicions.

Another questionable event in Ann Haskins' background was the way her adoptive parents died. House fires weren't particularly rare. Over three thousand deaths were caused by house fires every year in the United States. What was unusual was how Ann saved herself by jumping into her bathtub and submerging herself in water. Ann's testimony to the investigators revealed that she claimed she had drawn a bath and then fell asleep prior to getting into the tub naked. (It titillated Giordano to imagine the firefighters finding this beautiful young woman naked in the bathtub.) Luckily for her, the only injury she sustained was a bruise on her leg when she slipped and fell prior to getting into the tub. Apparently, she left her robe and her pajamas on top of the bed prior to entering the bathroom. *Why would she take the time to remove her clothes before getting into the bathtub to save herself?*

He noted with interest that the insurance adjuster who investigated the mysterious blaze had done a background check on Mr. and Mrs. Haskins and their daughter Ann. The investigator discovered that Ann Haskins worked at a strip club for several weeks following the fire. One of her dancer friends told the investigator that Ann told her that Mr. Elliot Haskins was a pervert. She also alleged that Ann let her know that Ann had been having regular sexual relations with her adoptive father for the past year. This information indicated that Ann Haskins had a clear motive to set the fire and kill her parents. However, there was no corroborative evidence and Ann denied those allegations. So, the matter was dropped and the insurance company paid off the claim.

However, when Giordano read the insurance inspector's notes concerning the cause of the fire, he found something else that piqued his interest. The cause of the fire was ruled to be the result of faulty wiring inside the wall leading to the window air-conditioner in the parents' bedroom. The gauge of the wire was inadequately sized for the amount of amperage the air-conditioner was pulling.

The investigator determined that the wiring was not original, but it appeared to have been done by a professional. Nothing sinister could be proven, so the claim was approved.

After spending more than a week reviewing all the various case materials and files Giordano was convinced that Ann Haskins was involved in her mother's murder, her boyfriend's accident, and she was probably guilty of murdering her adoptive parents as well. The problem was he couldn't prove anything. The cases were cold and most of the witnesses had long since disappeared or passed away. If Michael was involved, that was obviously a dead end, literally. Ann was the sole survivor of the Haskins family and the Trettin family.

Another thing he had dismissed at the time, but had nagged at him was the strange odor in Ann's garden. He recalled how the smell reminded him of decomposing human flesh, which seemed odd, since it was mixed with the sweet and fragrant smell of the flowers. No judge would grant a search warrant merely based on a mysterious smell, even if the odor was detected by the nose of an investigator renowned for his acute sense of smell. Unless, of course, there was a missing body that might be found lying in her front lawn. Giordano began an exhaustive search to find a missing person who recently vanished in a 150-mile radius around Nettleton. With the combined resources of the BSU and the Mississippi State police Giordano was able to identify several missing persons in the Alabama/Mississippi area.

Next, he needed to determine a likely M.O. Giordano

thought Ann might have assumed the role of a prostitute to lure men into a murderous web. Prostitution was a theme running through Ann's life. She had witnessed her mother's activities during her childhood. Ann had stripped and briefly worked as a prostitute herself. Some of her brother's victims were prostitutes.

Fortunately, Giordano didn't have to wait long for the investigators to come up with an actual missing person that could be a likely victim. Mr. Lance Redstone was a traveling salesman. Before his disappearance he had told his associate, he was going into a roadside tavern to get a beer and something to eat. He promised to join his associate later back at the motel. Mr. Redstone failed to appear the following day and his associate got worried and reported him missing. Two days later his two-door sedan was found out of gas on a deserted roadway off Highway 50 near Columbus, Mississippi. The officer who found the vehicle claimed there was no sign of a struggle and the car looked as if it had been abandoned. After canvassing several nearby taverns and clubs, a state policeman interviewed a bartender who thought he had seen the missing man. When he was shown the man's picture, the bartender immediately confirmed seeing the missing salesman. He described his companion as an attractive, petite blond with distinctive blue eyes. He thought she looked to be in her late thirties, forty at most.

Giordano decided that he had enough evidence to get a search warrant for Ann Haskins' property. If the body was found, the case would be solved and Ann would undoubtedly be convicted of killing the salesman. If no body or other evidence was found, well, at least she would be on the radar of the local police and eventually she might get caught for some other crime. Either way, he liked his odds.

When he presented his findings to both Larcovic and Bouldon he could tell they were pleased and impressed. It wasn't too hard to figure out that Ann Haskins, once you knew her profile, would likely turn out to be a criminal. She had an abusive mother, who was an alcoholic and the town whore. Ann may well have followed the example of her mother, but in a different way, just like her brother. She undoubtedly hated her mother, and like Michael, had learned to be both deceitful and cruel. Giordano was convinced that Ann had learned how to hide those traits by masquerading as a shy, innocent, naive, and damaged human being. Her attractive looks added another layer to her charade. Giordano told Larcovic that he didn't think Ann was insane. Far from it; he thought she was diabolically evil, just like her brother. Larcovic agreed that her profile predicted exactly what Giordano suspected.

* * *

A joint FBI and Mississippi State police task force arrived at the home of Ann Haskins with a search warrant the following morning at 6:00 a.m. Thirty minutes later, while digging into the garden, officers began uncovering bodies in various stages of decomposition. One of the officers joked with black humor that it appeared these men had unwillingly taken up residence in the garden.

Ann Haskins was arrested and immediately driven to the Tupelo jail. Surprisingly, without hesitation or remorse, Ann gave a detailed statement about the bodies found in her garden. It seemed as though she finally expected to be caught. Before the arrest, Ann made no attempt to flee or hide.

* * *

After the conviction of Ann Haskins six months later on two counts of murder, Agent Francis Albert Giordano was awarded the Meritorious Service Medal by Director Underwood. Giordano was credited for distinguished and outstanding service and accomplishments within the FBI and the BSU. After the award service concluded, Roger Bouldon approached Giordano and said, "I'd like to congratulate you for solving this case. It was brilliant work and I'm so glad you were recognized for your accomplishments. You know, from the very beginning I had my doubts about you, but you definitely proved me wrong. You're a great and resourceful agent and it has been a pleasure working with you professionally and getting to know you personally."

"Thank you, Roger!" Giordano said with feeling. "I will never let you, the FBI, or the BSU down. Always remember that. My only regret is I couldn't prove Ms. Haskins guilty of killing her mother, rigging her boyfriend's brakes, and killing her adoptive parents. I know she did it, but there just isn't enough evidence to charge her."

"Well Frank, if it weren't for your sensitive nose, Ms. Haskins might have gotten away with murder."

After a splutter of laughter, Giordano said, "I guess you're right. I finally found something useful about the size of my snout. Sinatra was famous for his singing. Maybe this will make me famous for my innate ability to smell death."

Bouldon chuckled and replied, "Yeah, they called Sinatra Old Blue Eyes. Maybe they'll call you Old Blue Nose."

They both laughed until they saw Larcovic approaching from the distance. He greeted both of his agents and then asked, "What's the joke?" But the two agents had resumed their professional appearance in the presence of their boss. "Come on guys, what were you talking about? We're off duty," Larcovic said with a smile.

Bouldon gave his boss a mock salute and responded senatorially, "How we're going to work more readily to solve the next case, Boss." But then turned serious and said, "We understand from the office rumor mill that we might be starting another serial murder investigation in Pennsylvania."

"That's correct. But for now, I'm glad to see you both celebrating this success. I'm planning to brief the team Monday morning. So be ready to travel!"